# Undivided

Stephanie Erickson

*For Shannon Mayer. Thank you for pointing me in the right direction. May the right "readers" always find you, my friend.*

# 1

"The unprecedented attack on London's British Museum is being called catastrophic. So far, twelve hundred people have died with another thousand unaccounted for. That number could have been much higher, but the day's low attendance was blamed on poor weather.

"The chemical has also done an unknown amount of damage to the priceless items on display within the museum. Exhibits from Ancient Egypt, Greece, Rome, and Australia have all sustained what authorities are calling 'significant and irreparable damage.'

"Authorities refer to the chemical as 'Zero,' and say the survival rate is based solely on proximity. Exposure to Zero shuts down the respiratory and endocrine systems, and those unlucky enough to be close to the toxin's point of release will die within four minutes of direct contact.

"ISIS is being blamed for the attack. However, the group's uncharacteristic denial of their involvement is breeding doubt for many politicians looking to point fingers. Normally, the terrorist organization claims responsibility for their attacks almost immediately. But, other politicians, like Department of Defense Secretary Chris Becker, claim there is no normal for terrorist organizations."

The brightly dressed, middle-aged anchorwoman faded from the screen. She was replaced with an overweight, balding gentleman dressed in a gray suit with a bright blue tie. He stood in front of a podium, clearly at a press conference, camera bulbs flashing on his face occasionally. "ISIS is a terrorist organization. Why should we take their word for anything? Terrorists can't be trusted." He shook a finger at the camera as he said it, driving his point home. Beneath his image, he was identified as Department of Defense Secretary Chris Becker.

The anchorwoman's voice rang out over the image. "Others say placing the blame on ISIS is a political stratagem intended to distract the public from the larger issue of whether or not this attack can be linked to the attack on Coda in Florida a few short weeks ago. There are fears that a new serial terrorist group might be at large.

"Many say the link is irrefutable, since both attacks were made with the same toxin. Others hesitate to make the connection without further evidence."

The image switched to a video feed of a man dressed in a full police uniform addressing a crowd from a podium. He was identified at the bottom of the screen as Chief Constable George Lindley. "The Ministry of Defense and I are not ready to jump to any conclusions until all the evidence regarding the attack on the London museum is properly analyzed."

The shot returned to the anchorwoman. "More as we get it. For now, I'm Lila Fox for NBC News Thirteen."

David muted the television, and we all went quiet. The oval-shaped table we sat around was brand new. Everything was new. We'd been relocated in the days following Coda. The Potestas had learned too much about our facility and how to access it, thanks to me. We'd settled into our new home deep in the mountains of Colorado almost three weeks ago, and I loved it. The crisp air and cooler temperatures were both wins in my book. But the Potestas were giving us no time to relax in our new digs.

"How did the authorities even pick up that term, Zero?" Owen asked via Skype. His voice was almost unrecognizable—an unfortunate side effect of the injuries he'd sustained in Coda. It was deep and raspy, almost like he'd spent sixty years smoking, even though he wasn't yet thirty. He was still recovering from his other injuries, but luckily for him, our new hospital ward was much nicer than the one at our old facility.

"Someone must have fed it to them." The comment just slipped out of my mouth. Zero was a term I'd heard the Potestas use while I was caught in their web. As far as I knew, we were the only other people who knew its name. Someone inside had to have told the right people what it was called. Either that or a member of the Potestas was doubling as a member of the authorities. The thought made my skin crawl, but I knew it wasn't outside the realm of possibility.

"It's a troubling thought," David said, tapping the table in front of him with his finger.

"The Ministry of Mind Reading in London issued a brief statement to us. They said they did get a little bit of intel, tipping them off to the attack, but it was too little, too late." David paused. "They didn't put the pieces together fast enough."

Rebecca, the replacement for Tracy, our fallen instructor, spoke up. "Owen, are you sure there was nothing at Coda marking the chemical? No indication of what it was?"

"Honestly? No. I never found the release device, let alone any canisters of the chemical. I was more concerned with getting people out. A lot of it is kind of a blur." Shrugging his bandaged shoulder without thinking, he tried to hide a wince. He was sitting up and talking, which was a vast improvement, but he still had a long way to go. I smiled encouragingly at him, but I was seated next to the computer monitor, so he couldn't see me anyway.

Mitchell was sitting on the other side of the computer, keeping quiet. Rebecca was next to him, while Camden and the others were scattered around the large, oval table. David sat directly across from the computer screen, so he had the best view of Owen. Not all the seats at the table were full, but all the remaining members of our team were there, about twenty of us total.

"From what I learned during my captivity—" I said, choking on the words. I hated to think of the time I'd spent in their power, "—the Potestas are working toward a 'position of power,' whatever that means. Knowing how they operate, I'd guess a different member of their ranks is in charge of each attack." I glanced at the screen behind David, which showed people scrambling in the streets out in front of the museum. "Clearly they're angling to be a global force. So, what can we do?" I asked.

"We can get to work," David said.

After our meeting, I made my way across our new facility to see Owen. Whereas our Florida home had been vertically aligned, our new home was horizontal. Built right into a mountain, it was perfectly concealed and very scenic. It was originally intended for a much larger division of Unseen members, but they were sent to Washington after the attack on Coda to bolster our efforts at headquarters.

We were situated deep in the Rocky Mountains, but a subtle tunnel ran from one of the small side roads to the main entrance, allowing us to get in and out as needed. Of course, several layers of security concealed the entrance, and we were located about twenty miles from the nearest town. I preferred to go out another way, through the smaller entrance that opened into the wilderness surrounding the mountain facility. We were inside the tree line, so the forest engulfed us, but it was only a short walk to a beautiful mountain lake that reflected the surrounding range as perfectly as if someone had painted it there.

It reminded me of the mountain lake in the mind prison Dylan Shields constructed for me, but not in a bad way. It was beautiful. Just as Mitchell still enjoyed eating ice cream sundaes after the Potestas had used them to torture his childhood self, I still appreciated our new home's beauty.

The inside of our new building was totally different from our Florida facility. For one thing, there was a lot more metal, including the walkway I was currently using. Our old home had been coated with thickly laid cement, intended to keep out the water and sand. Here, the builders seemed to have used steel beams and rods to hold the mountain up around us. In some places, they'd even left the rock exposed, and I loved to run my hands along its cool surface as I walked by.

The air was cool and dry inside because of the altitude, and I went through about a gallon of moisturizer a day. But it was a nice feeling, particularly since I was used to the thick humidity of Florida.

Owen hadn't warmed to our new home the way I had. Of course, he was still in a chemical coma when we left Florida, so when he woke up, the changes were jarring to say the least. Add his injuries to that insult, and his mood was thoroughly sour. But as I breathed in the cool, refreshing air, I felt confident Owen would come to love it as much as I did. He just needed time to adjust.

When I arrived at the hospital wing, I rested my hand against a panel on the wall to be scanned, and the door opened inward, allowing me passage. Although the flooring was made of metal grates, and the walls were literally carved out of the mountainside, the equipment was the same as it had been at home, giving the room a familiar feel.

Staff was sparse down there. Owen was their only patient for the moment, but there were enough beds to treat all of us if something catastrophic happened. I nodded to a nurse who was filling one of the drawers with supplies as I walked toward Owen's room. I didn't need to hear what she was thinking to know she was a reader. All employees of the Unseen were.

I knocked on his door, but I didn't wait for him to respond before I opened it and walked in. No way was I allowing him to stew alone in his crankiness.

Despite being several hundred feet inside a mountain, the room was well lit. They'd used natural bulbs instead of fluorescent lights, which gave it a homier feel, and there was even a plant in the corner, along with some chairs, a state-of-the-art smart TV, and a private bathroom with a spa-like tub that his injuries did not allow him to use. If you ignored the equipment and hospital bed, which gave the room an undeniably sterile feel, it was quite nice.

"Hey," I said, making my way around to the chair next to his bed. He nodded at me, but he said nothing.

Bandages still covered both his arms and his left shoulder, but his wounds had stopped oozing, so at least they looked clean. And he was sitting up, facing the TV, so that was another step in the right direction. Currently, it was on mute, which was a promising sign that he'd be willing to talk. His beautiful, black hair was greasy and lackluster from going too long without washing, and his face had taken on a yellow hue, but to me, he was more handsome than ever. After all, he'd loved me in my darkest hour, and looking down at him, I knew it wouldn't be hard to return the favor.

"What do you think?" I asked.

"We have grossly underestimated them. Once we accept that, we can start to move forward."

"Yes, I suppose you're right. But I think David is hoping for a more glass-is-half-full outcome."

"Then he's a fool." Combined with his rough new voice, it came out shockingly cold.

"Owen," I said, a bit of scolding in my tone. Owen used to consider my father something of a hero, which I'd always struggled to understand, but this level of disrespect swung too far the other way.

Finally, he looked into my eyes. "You know it's true. They're attacking, and we're sitting here doing nothing. Nothing but harboring useless monsters like me and vigilantes like you," he said.

"Hey. That's enough." His comment stung, even if it was deserved. Yes, I had gone after one of my best friend's killers on my own, but that seemed like such a long time ago now. So much had changed in a few short weeks. I looked at Owen's bandaged body, at the evidence of all the hurt we'd both suffered, and hoped we'd make it to the other side of this battle without losing any more of ourselves.

"It's not enough until we start to fight back," he said.

Where was my positive, patient, and loving man? Damned if I wasn't going to find him buried under all those bandages. "Well, you know what? I'm starting with you. This attitude stops now. You've been nothing but this angry, kinda bratty version of yourself since you woke up, and I'm tired of it. Snap out of it."

"Well, how would you feel? I thought I was doing the right thing, Mac. I risked my life to save those people, just like we're supposed to do, and this was the thanks I got." He held up his bandaged arms and let them fall heavily back to the bed, wincing as they hit.

"Your life was the thanks you got."

"And was your life any comfort to you when your mind was trapped in the psyche of Dylan Shields?" His tone had a self-righteous note to it that I didn't like.

"Stop it. Now you're just being mean. This isn't you."

"Don't tell me what is and isn't me." He was being so cold, but I kept reminding myself not to take it personally. He was in mourning. But he hadn't lost a friend or a loved one. He'd lost himself.

I wanted to take his hand, but the bandages meant I could not even give him that simple comfort. Instead, I rested my hand on his leg. The stony look in his dark eyes told me he wasn't about to listen, but I had to try. "*You* don't know who you are right now. And that's okay." He didn't relax in my grasp, but he didn't pull away either.

He turned his head away from me, and when he next spoke, his voice was sad and tired. "You don't understand."

"You're right, I don't. And you don't understand the things I went through, the things Mitchell went through, or hell, the things Tracy went through. But I'll tell you what I do know. You were my rock after I lost my best friend. Now my rock has turned into a solitary statue, thinking he can withstand every storm on his own. And who knows, maybe you're right. After all, if you're my rock, what am I to you?"

He looked at me then, some of the softness returning. "You don't need a rock anymore, Mac. And you certainly don't need a monster. You should find someone else."

Oddly, his words didn't hurt me. I knew deep down it was only his grief talking. That was something I understood all too well.

"Who else would tolerate me?" I chuckled. "Who else would tolerate *you*?" But he didn't laugh like I hoped he would.

"Well, if you're going to keep calling yourself a monster, maybe I'll change your name to Oscar, since you're such a grouch all the time." The corner of his mouth lifted just a hair, but it was enough to tell me he was still in there under all that grief and anger.

"Mac, you know they'll strike again."

"Mmhmm. But Dr. Jeppe just finished the formula a few months ago. They can't possibly have it in mass quantities yet. Besides, the Unseen in Washington are hot on their trail. There's bound to be a breakthrough soon."

"Don't underestimate them," he warned, looking down at his mangled body.

"Owen, that's not what you did. What happened

wasn't your fault. And if you hadn't been there, thousands more people would have died. Think of all the families you saved from heartache. Don't you see how heroic your efforts actually were?"

"I suppose you're right. But the cost was high."

"It always is," I said, thinking of Dylan Shields. In order to save the members of the Unseen, I killed the man who'd imprisoned me in his mind. He had a son—an infant, as far as I could tell.

Knowing he wouldn't take what I had to say next lightly, I braced myself. "David is anxious to get me back to work, now that you're..." I hesitated, not wanting to draw attention to his current state. "Doing better. Starting tomorrow, Rebecca and I are going to begin developing some stronger techniques to overcome the Potestas. Do you remember her?" I couldn't bring myself to say her title out loud. Tracy's death was still too fresh.

He nodded. "She stopped by once or twice. Seems nice. Left a couple of little stuffed animals around."

Searching, I quickly spotted her crocheted creations on the table next to his bed. One was Chewbacca, and the other was Jabba the Hut. The thoughtful gesture made me smile. *Star Wars* was Owen's all-time favorite movie. "She's a lot different than Tracy, but I like her. You might also be interested to know Mitchell seems to like her quite a bit."

"Really?" He couldn't hide his curiosity, which made me smile. It was good to see him engaged, even if it was over gossip. Our strong, silent friend had taken quite a shining to the bubbly, outgoing woman, and it was the first time I'd seen him express such an interest in anyone. She was his opposite in almost every way, but somehow, they seemed perfect for each other. This was good stuff.

"Mmmhmm. I left them sitting on the couch when I came down here. They were nearly touching."

He nodded to himself, looking more relaxed. Any other time, he would've smiled. Instead, he simply said, "Good." I accepted his answer, knowing it would have to do for now.

"Anyway, David hopes we can train the others. That way, we'll be better prepared for the next…" The next what? Attack? Ambush? Mission? Hopefully not the next mistake. "The next time. There are a lot of things we need to work through."

"Sounds like." He didn't hide the sadness in his voice.

"Listen, don't think you'll get out of helping us while you're in here. I'm going to be over here constantly to pick your brain and ask for pointers. You've been here longer than me, so you better be ready to contribute."

He perked up a little, and I thought I saw a flash of the old mischief in his eyes. He held up his bandaged arms. "I'm just an invalid. I need to rest."

I dramatically rolled my eyes and sighed. Picking up the remote and pointing it at Owen, I said, "This channel is getting boring. How do I change it?"

He snatched it from me and unmuted the television. We watched in companionable silence for a long time, but I didn't even register what was on. I was too wrapped up in my thoughts about Owen, Zero, Shields, and the Potestas' quest for power. They'd already proven they were willing to take lives without mercy or apology in pursuit of their goal, and somehow, I was caught up in the middle of it.

As I sat there with Owen, I had no idea what I could or would do about any of it, but unlike the girl I had been, who'd been so lost in mourning for Maddie she could barely function, I knew I *would* do something. I wouldn't bury myself in that haze of depression ever again. I would take control of this situation, affect a change, and be Unseen. And Owen would do the same, if I had anything to say about it.

# 2

Our new training facility was top of the line, not that we had wanted for anything before. But this was different. All the equipment was brand new, complete with digital screens that measured everything from the efficiency of your workout to caloric burn and heart rate, as well as big screen TVs that broadcasted workout videos and displayed how certain equipment should be used. But the pièce de résistance was an incredible system of holographic trainers. You wore headphones when you exercised with one of them, so only you could hear your trainer, and the hologram could be tailored to meet your needs. You could make it a man or a woman, a drill sergeant or more of a hand holder, whatever your preference. It was odd to walk through the gym and see all the holograms pointing, gesturing, getting in people's faces, and sometimes even working out alongside them.

Even the training rooms seemed nicer. They were much larger, with digital white boards instead of actual white boards, and plush chairs. These rooms were built for use, unlike the small, cell-like rooms I trained in with Tracy. I found myself actually looking forward to the long days ahead.

A pang of guilt washed over me, and I thought of how excited Tracy would've been to see the new facility, and how she and I would've put everything to good use. But she wasn't here, and she never would be again. I'd failed to properly protect her—or myself—in our confrontation with Dylan Shields. I sighed as I crossed the open gym, filled with people who were either lifting weights or working out with a holographic trainer. She wouldn't have wanted me to mope around. She would've wanted me to get to work.

As I put my hand on the door to the training room where I'd arranged to meet Rebecca, I decided that was exactly what I would do.

"I suppose there's no better place to start than the beginning," Rebecca said, tucking a strand of long, wavy brown hair behind her ear. "I know Tracy was a bit guarded about her personal life, but you know I don't operate like that. We've spent a fair amount of time together over the past few weeks, but we haven't shared too many details about ourselves yet. What with the move, Owen's recovery, and the new attack, there just hasn't been time to get down to the nitty-gritty of who we are. Now's the time to change that!" She smiled as she said it, as if the prospect of obliterating this social boundary between us excited her.

"I'm almost thirty, so I've been working with The Unseen for over fifteen years—gosh, is that right?" She thought for a moment, looking a bit wistful. "Yeah, it is. Makes me feel old." She chuckled. "My family died when I was young. Believe it or not, it was of natural causes." Perhaps in some conversations, this disclaimer would be unusual, but many members of the Unseen had lost family to the Potestas. While the two organizations were both large groups of organized mind readers, the Potestas often worked for their own personal gain, while the Unseen strived for justice as best as they could. As a result, many members of the Unseen had lost their families in the struggles.

"They were older anyway," she continued. "I was their miracle child—their one and only. Dad went first, and Mom followed not long after. They were both in their seventies, but I was barely a teenager, so I couldn't cope. The Unseen found me and took me in.

"You know, I met Tracy years ago, in a training meeting. We were learning the latest training techniques and brainstorming methods of sharpening our forces. She was formidable, even then." She smiled at the memory, and I smiled right along with her. Formidable was the perfect adjective for Tracy. "She kept her distance, but I liked her. Her knowledge and skills were impressive. I knew she had a lot to offer, so I aligned myself with her right away. I could never tell if she found me charming or annoying."

"Probably both," I said with a chuckle.

Her smile warmed me, gave me hope somehow. "I don't mind telling you that I'm very excited about getting to work with *the* Mackenzie Day. I can't wait to see what we can teach each other."

It was refreshing to be around her, energizing even. I found myself sitting forward in my seat, just as excited as she was to get to work. I hadn't told Owen, not wanting to reinforce his dark mood, but I completely understood his distaste for stagnation. My fingers twitched with the desire to move, to help, to make music of the mind.

"All right, let's get started. Tell me what they did to trap you in Shields's mind, what the prison was like, and how you think we can use it to our advantage."

"I can tell you until I'm blue in the face, but I think it would be better to show you." If Tracy had taught me one lesson, it was that. And now that I'd been through hell, I wasn't as frightened of it. I was strong enough to show her what had been done to me without hurting her. I always had been—the difference was that now I knew it.

As soon as I allowed her into my mind, I created a prison for her. Though I had been free of Shields' prison for weeks now, the idea of it still captivated me, as if holding me in its thrall. I often imagined what a prison of my own creation would be like, and who might occupy it. I never imagined putting my imaginings into practice, particularly not on a friend. But she needed to see what we were up against.

Swallowing hard, I captured her in our own little prison. I tried to make it pleasant, with plenty of crocheting supplies, a lovely view similar to the mountainside we now occupied, and several dashing pictures of Mitchell scattered around. This last detail made me smile to myself.

At first, she didn't touch anything; she just stood still, her eyes slowly examining her surroundings. Then she started to explore. It was odd for me to be on the other side, watching her, knowing Shields had watched me the same way. The thought gave me the willies. "All right, you get the idea," I said, ready to stop.

"No, not yet," she said, her voice distant, like she was deep in thought. She started to walk around, running her hands over the piles of yarn as she went. "This is nice yarn. Very high quality."

"I thought you'd want the best."

"Mmm." Moving over to the windows, she stood there for a moment, taking in the mountain view. She stood there for several moments.

Suddenly, something occurred to me. The projection screens that had been such a huge part of my hell were missing from Rebecca's prison. While I was in Shields' mind, those screens had served as my only connection to my body and the outside world. How had they shown those to me?

"I think for you to be able to see the projection screen I saw—the one that showed me what my body was seeing—someone else would have to take control of your body. But I could also see what Shields was seeing on a separate screen. That's how they showed me they had me." I let the comment drop off, as I considered how I could show her what I was looking at without freeing her from the prison.

The only method that seemed to make sense was for me to open my eyes. So I did. And it severed our connection less than gracefully.

We both moaned and I doubled over, holding my head in my hands and bracing myself on my knees.

"What happened?" Her question was muffled behind her hands.

"I opened my eyes."

"Why?" It wasn't a why-is-the-grass-green kind of why, but more of a why-on-Earth-would-you-do-such-a-thing kind of why.

"Because I was trying to show you what the projection screens looked like. I wanted you to have the full experience, and I figured it could also help us understand what they'd done from the other side. Maybe we can use some of this."

She nodded. "Maybe." I could tell by her tone there was more to that maybe. What did she know that I didn't? But I didn't push it. She'd voice her mind when she was ready.

"Put me back in the prison," she said.

"What? Why?" I asked, fairly certain I wasn't ready to do what she'd requested. My head still ached from our last attempt.

"Because I want to try to find a way out. You can tinker with the projection if you want." But it was more of an afterthought, something to keep me busy while she did the real work.

I chuckled. "If I want?"

"Well, seems to me like it was a focus and control issue that broke our connection so...abruptly. Everyone could benefit from working on those two things. Give it a go."

So, we settled in and got back to work.

She wandered around the prison, quietly taking everything in, and I tried to concentrate on focus and control. Twice more, I broke our connection. By midday, we both had raging headaches.

"Do you want to press on? I feel like my nose is going to start bleeding at any moment," I said, cradling my head in my hands.

"Yes, let's keep at it. Remember, the pain isn't real," she said with a smile on her face.

"That's a load of BS, and you know it. Every time I touched Tracy's fence, it shocked the hell out of me."

"You touched it more than once? Sounds like you're a pretty slow learner." She couldn't even get it out without smiling.

"Fine," I said, rather indignant. "Let's just get back to work."

But the pain in my head was becoming overwhelming. While she just meandered around, concentrating and focusing were becoming more and more difficult because of the pounding. *It's not real*, I told myself. It didn't help. The pounding still kept a rhythm with my heartbeat, but instead of ignoring it, I used it. It was a steady beat, almost like a metronome. Instinctually, I started remembering how Gaspard de la Nuit went, letting my heart sing the tune.

When my eyes came open this time, I managed to hold on to our connection.

"This is a little overwhelming," Rebecca said in my head. She sat in front of me silently, eyes closed, head bowed, not speaking. And yet, I could hear her voice clearly and feel her moving around inside my prison. I knew exactly what she was doing without closing my eyes, almost as if I existed in two realities at once.

"What part is overwhelming for you?"

"The music, seeing myself sitting in that chair. It's all

really odd." Her voice was a bit distant, almost as if I'd created space between us by opening my eyes.

"You can hear the music too?"

"Yes. It's a lovely tune. In fact, it sounds a lot like the one you were playing the night we met. It's just a bit much at the moment. It would be good for a foe though. Anything to throw them off-guard."

Watching her body take slow but steady breaths, I grew increasingly unsettled. I didn't like having her locked away inside my mind.

"Great, another weapon for the enemy. You about done? This is really uncomfortable. It's like watching you sleep sitting up."

"I suppose I am dreaming, in a sense," she said as she continued to run her hands over random objects in the house I'd created for her. "Dreams are nothing more than a different state of consciousness, right? Here I am, active, alive, and well, just not inside my body.

"But what does it take to wake up? Is the only way out of this for me to kill you?" she asked suddenly.

"Don't get hasty. I can let you out, too." I'd meant it as a joke, but it wasn't really funny. "Yes," I added after letting out an uncomfortable chuckle. "It was the only way I could get out. Maybe someone else could find a more elegant solution, but I was feeling pressed for time."

"No, no. I'm not criticizing you. I'm just assessing the options." She baffled me. Tracy never would've said such a thing to me. She was always criticizing, always trying to improve, but Rebecca took a totally different approach.

As she walked around her prison, she smiled at a picture of Mitchell before moving on. "These are a nice touch, by the way," she said, barely above a whisper.

"You know, when Owen and I started dating, everyone knew about it. It bothered me to no end that I didn't know how to guard my thoughts. But I guess it didn't matter much; you're not broadcasting your thoughts, and everyone knows you and Mitchell hit it off."

Her laugh helped me relax. "No, I suppose it didn't matter at all," she said, taking one more look at the picture of Mitchell before setting it back down.

She spent what little time was left in the day unsuccessfully trying to find a way to escape.

When I finally pushed her out at the end of the day, she was shaken. She pushed her chair away from me just a tiny bit, enough for me to feel the larger space between us. "That was a truly terrible experience. I knew it wouldn't be permanent; it was just weird to be so absolutely trapped. This could be an excellent self-defense mechanism when dealing with an adversary, Mac. You could trap an enemy until reinforcements arrive, or until you get away…" She trailed off, mentally ticking off all possible applications for the tactic.

"Right, but it's dangerous. If you can't keep them in the prison, you risk giving them control of your mind or worse. Plus, the concentration it takes to do anything in the real world while keeping someone trapped in your mind is ridiculous." I paused as I considered the realistic possibilities this technique might have for us. "It's not perfect."

"No, nothing is," she said as she gathered her things. "But it's a start." She squeezed my shoulder and left the room.

In the days that followed, Rebecca pushed me in a way Tracy never had. She created fake or unimportant memories for me to destroy, told me how it felt, and then showed me how to do it better. Her method was much more elegant than mine—she almost dissolved them instead of just crushing them and moving on. We practiced control, pushing each other out, reading each other's thoughts, everything. But I still felt like we were one step behind the Potestas. These were all things they already knew how to do.

While Rebecca and I were sequestered in our own

little world, everyone else was buried in research on the Potestas. Our division had been charged with finding as much information as possible to help those in the Unseen's Washington headquarters. While we worked in the training rooms, Mitchell and the others were scouring the Internet, secure databases, and any other intel they could hack into for everything they could find out about Zero, its location and quantities, where it might be unleashed next, and who would be responsible for doing it.

One day, toward the end of the week, we were sitting in the training room just looking at each other, when a question occurred to me. "What do you typically need on a mission?"

"Well, focus…and sometimes reinforcements."

"Right. But you don't always know you need reinforcements until you're knee deep in it, right?"

"Right…" She trailed off, not quite understanding what I was getting at.

"And reinforcements often take too long to arrive. You're left to make decisions for yourself on the fly."

"Yes. Thinking on your feet is an important skill for our agents."

"But what if we could hear one another and communicate while we're out on missions?" I stood up and paced around the room as the idea worked itself out in my head.

"Well, that would be very useful. You could have direct access to the researchers for more information, or to David for advice and help. Or you could talk someone through a tight spot."

"But there would be drawbacks."

"Like what?" she asked, clearly not ready to stop listing the positives.

"Well, if you were captured, it could theoretically create a direct line for the Potestas to everyone here."

Her mouth opened, and then shut as she leaned back

in her chair, all the excitement draining out of her.

"Now, I don't think we should abandon the idea entirely. I just think we need to come up with a failsafe—a way to hide or defend the connection in the event of danger. Much like the way we protect our own minds."

"All missions are dangerous, Mac. Every time we leave the compound, we risk getting caught."

I nodded. "All the more reason to have as many reinforcements as possible, don't you think?"

That night, I rushed to the hospital wing to see Owen, excited to share my idea with him. I'd been to see him every night, but I felt different tonight. No amount of his gloom could bring me down.

I bounded into his room and started in immediately. "What do you think of this idea? What if we were able to communicate internally even when we weren't in the same room, when we were out on assignment, say?"

He thought for a moment, and I felt heartened by the fact he was actually considering my question. "Well, I'd say that would be a pretty helpful skill. Particularly since it seems like I'm never going to get out of this hospital bed for any respectable length of time. I fear I may melt and meld with the bed."

"Then you really would be a Sesame Street monster. I'm pretty sure Bert and Ernie had a talking bed at one point."

Instead of laughing, he morosely stared at the ceiling. "Hey, I heard they were going to let you go up to your room soon," I said, changing gears. "What happened to that?"

"Soon. That's what happened. They won't give me a date. They won't say if soon means tomorrow or next week. I'm sick of being in here. I want out. I want to work with you guys. I want to be part of this."

His frustration was plain on his face, and I think if he could have reached for something, he would've thrown it.

I sighed. "Owen, you have a long, hard road ahead of you. Why are you so eager to start walking on it, when you should be resting and building up your strength for the journey?"

"Isn't that poetic?" The contempt in his voice stung, and it must've shown on my face, because he softened a bit. "The sooner I start walking the road, the sooner I come out on the other side. That's all."

I moved to his bedside and sat down. "That's probably true. But the stronger you are, the further you'll be able to walk. Please," I begged. "Anyway, just yesterday, you were whining about therapy being too much work. Sounds like your taskmaster nurse won't let you 'meld with the bed,' if you ask me."

He chuckled a little, and the sound made my heart sing. "She must've taken a page from Tracey's book. She's merciless."

"It's good for you. Builds character," I said, wanting to take his hand but still unsure if I could touch his brand-new skin. Instead, I rested my hand near his, so our fingers—his peeking out of his bandages—barely touched. He'd been doing therapy in some form since before he woke up. At first, it was just the nurse moving his body around. But now, they were making him move himself, walk, lift things, pushing him to his limits every day, but on a much more basic—and frustrating—level than what Rebecca and I were doing.

He was quiet for a moment. "The world is collapsing to chaos around us. And I can barely get my pants down to go to the bathroom by myself." I knew he was talking about the attack at the British Museum. The last of the memorials had been held, and ISIS still refused to take responsibility. The media's resolve that ISIS was responsible was starting to crumble, but no one else was stepping forward to claim it. Half the general public's panic was a result of a very understandable fear of the unknown. Of course, we knew who was responsible, and worse, that they'd strike again before this was over, which didn't help me rest any easier than the average Joe.

"Owen, this is talk for another day. A day when there aren't so many other things to worry about."

"There will always be other things to worry about. Why shouldn't we worry about the lives of thousands of people today? Just because I'm lying in a hospital bed with injuries from the very chemical the Potestas are using to attack innocent people?"

"I just meant that there are other people who are dealing with this situation. Today, you're not one of them. Maybe you will be tomorrow, but for now, this isn't your concern."

That turned his mood even darker. "It *should* be my concern. Of everyone here, I know firsthand what Zero can do. I should be helping to stop it." He paused for a moment, considering what to say. "Mackenzie, this is bigger than you or me. I don't mean to sound dramatic, but this toxin could be used to end the world as we know it. They're going to need every one of us to stop it. This is no time for me to act like an invalid. Every second counts in this battle. I should be helping."

"You are. You will. You've been included in all the meetings via Skype. Please be content with helping us in that capacity until you can help yourself. You need to concentrate your energy on your recovery, instead of focusing on all the bad things in life," I begged. His mood was starting to worry me. "Seriously Owen, soon is better than never. And soon, you'll be out of here and back in action."

"Soon might as well be never," he muttered, but even though I understood his frustration, I ignored him. Honestly, I didn't know what else to do. I wasn't sure how to help him. All I could do was hope.

On my way back to my room, I found Mitchell watching TV with Rebecca. They were sitting on the couch together, their legs just barely touching. I smiled to myself and cleared my throat. "Mitchell. A word?"

Rebecca smiled as he got up, and the complete adoration I saw in her eyes made it even more difficult to hide a grin of my own.

We maneuvered the main walkway to the secondary door, then went out and sat near the edge of the lake. It took the better part of three minutes to make our way outside, but we didn't speak.

The night sky was filled with thousands of stars, more than I'd ever seen when I lived in Florida. Light pollution there made it impossible to see so many systems. But in the shadow of the mountains around us, stars shone so brightly it seemed like I could reach up and grab a handful of them.

Taking a deep breath, I told Mitchell what was on my mind. "I'm worried about Owen."

"Mmhmm," he said, looking out over the water as he picked at a long piece of grass.

"I think his attitude is hurting his recovery."

"Agreed."

"What can we do?" I asked, not considering for a moment that the man next to me wouldn't have an answer. He knew Owen like a brother. He would know how to help.

"Nothing, really. He'll come out of it on his own, when he's ready."

"But what if he doesn't?"

"And he goes on a killing rampage?" He looked sidelong at me, and I smacked him. Regardless of whether or not what I'd done to Washington had been right, or just, I'd never live it down.

"Well!" I said with a hint of indignation.

"We both came through our ordeals okay. He will too. Just give him time." He stood up and brushed the grass off his pants, but I wasn't quite ready. The man I loved was hurting. I couldn't just sit idly by while he wasted away.

"With everything that's going on, I'm not sure he'll get the time he needs." Owen was right. The Potestas were on the move, and it was only a matter of time before their real intentions were revealed.

"Well, maybe that'll be the kick in the pants he needs, hmm?" He held his hand out to me and hoisted me onto my feet. Apparently, we were done talking, whether I liked it or not.

"He's already had a pretty good kick in the pants," I said, almost under my breath. We were quiet as we made our way back to the door, so I wasn't sure he'd heard me.

He came to a stop on the path and turned to face me. "Listen, Owen is wired differently than you and me. Even though his whole family died around him, he wasn't bitter. He's…" He trailed off.

"He's more forgiving," I filled in. I had reason to know. Considering the self-righteous way I'd acted after discovering the Unseen's true purpose—that we existed to wipe out terrorists before they could carry out their murderous plots—Owen had forgiven me rather quickly for taking justice into my own hands with one of Maddie's killers.

Mitchell nodded as we went back inside. "He'll come around, you'll see."

I followed him back into the living room, where Rebecca welcomed him with a glowing smile, and I couldn't help but notice the glimmer in his eyes as he reclaimed his seat next to her.

He'd been broken once, but you wouldn't know it to look at him. That could happen for Owen too. And it would. Soon, I hoped.

In the meantime, all I had to do was find a way to save the world from Zero. The weight of it made me hunch over a little as I made my way to my room.

"Sure. No problem. Just save the world," I said as I leaned on the inside of my bedroom door, in the middle of a mountain, where no one could hear me.

# 3

Rebecca and I worked through the weekend, trying to establish a strong, stable connection between us that would not sever at a distance. It was frustrating at first. She could hear me, and I could hear her just fine, but as soon as we got out of range, it was over. And our range was frustratingly short. Only a few yards if we couldn't see each other, further if we could. But the whole point was to be able to do it over thousands of miles.

By Sunday night, we were both feeling a little defeated. We sat in the training room in silence, each staring off into our own world.

I was so burned out from the last forty-eight hours, I wasn't really thinking about anything at all. But still, I reached out lazily for nothing in particular. It was then I noticed Rebecca's mind was recognizable, unique. Her mind had a signature, so to speak. It felt warm and bubbly. It packed everything that made her *her* into this tiny little ball of light, feeling, and energy. What would happen if I hung on to that signature as I moved farther away from her?

*Hey*, I thought as I stood up.
*Hey yourself. Where ya going?*

*Just roll with me.*

*You got it, especially if it means I get to stay here.* She leaned back in her chair and rested her head against the wall.

*Don't fall asleep!*

*You're quite the taskmaster.* She gave me a wink as I walked out of the training room and closed the door behind me.

I walked all the way across the floor before I tried to speak to her. But I knew it would work, because I could still feel her. Her signature stood out to me now.

*Still there?*

*Yeah, where are you?* she asked

*Heading toward the kitchen.*

*You've done it!*

*Maybe.* I didn't want to jump the gun, so I kept walking. I wasn't sure when I would feel sure that I had, in fact, done it, but two rooms over wasn't instilling enough confidence to stake a mission on our ability to train the others in this newfound skill.

Once I was outside, I tried again. *It's nice out tonight. Getting pretty cold.*

*Are you outside?*

*No, I'm just checking the weather on my phone. Of course I'm outside,* I teased.

*This is amazing! Come back in here and tell me how to do it!*

Her enthusiasm made me pick up my pace as I headed back toward the training room. I'd done it. I'd created a connection to another mind that could withstand distance. The question was—could I repeat it?

On my way back to the training room, I grabbed David. Just like in our old place, his new office was near the training rooms, and I wondered if that placement was standard in all Unseen facilities. I knocked on his door and popped my head inside.

"You busy?"

He looked up from some files. His new space was

bigger, with a huge, modern black desk in the center of the room. There were two big, black cabinets with frosted glass doors on the top half of the wall and massive file drawers on the bottom behind him. I wondered if one of them was the door to his apartment, or if that was hidden somewhere else in the room. "That depends on what you want." By the look of his smile, his threat was empty.

"Can you help us out for a second?"

"Oh, sure. I'll be there in just a moment." He gathered his papers together, and I left him to it, knowing he'd follow soon.

*What's taking you so long?* Rebecca asked just as I was walking back into the room.

"I wanted reinforcements to see if I can duplicate the experiment. The results are nothing but coincidence unless you can reliably duplicate them."

"I didn't know you were such a scientist."

I was too excited to acknowledge her quip. "Once we've done that, we need to figure out how to protect the connection. Then I can teach you how to do it. But not before. That way we won't risk you getting inadvertently captured and exposing all of us."

She frowned. "Well, I don't have any dangerous kamikaze missions on my calendar yet, but if one pops up, you'll be the first to know."

She ignored my laughter, reluctantly relenting. "You're right, of course. But aren't I the one who's in charge of training?"

My smile turned mischievous. "Are you?"

She threw a wad of paper at me just as David walked in.

"David. This is a nice surprise," she said, and I could tell she meant it.

"Mackenzie asked me to pop in."

I nodded toward him. "Duplicate," I said to Rebecca.

"Ah. Good. This will be fun," she said, but David looked skeptical.

"The last time I helped you with your training, Tracy nearly got lost in your head. I'm not sure what you have in mind, but I'd rather not be your guinea pig."

"Come on, you big chicken." His skeptical expression made me push a little harder. "Da-vid, please?" I stumbled over his name because *Dad* was on the tip of my tongue, but I held the word back. I didn't relish the idea of calling him Dad for the first time to manipulate him into doing things my way.

He sighed heavily. "Fine. But I swear, if something happens to me, you do *not* want to be in charge of this place. These kids are a bunch of renegade vigilantes," he said to Rebecca.

"I prefer spirited, loyal individuals, but whatever. Also, we're not kids." Of course, David hadn't known me when I was a kid. Back then, I'd been more of a rule follower.

He looked at me with a bit of nostalgia in his eyes. "You are to me."

Rebecca chuckled. "Aw. That's sweet." She knew David was my father just like everyone else in our group did. His secret had stopped being…well, *secret*, the minute he invited me to join the Unseen.

"Just get it over with," he grumbled

Reaching out for him, I felt for his signature. I could still pinpoint Rebecca, which I took as a positive. But David was harder to pick out. Maybe it was because he was my dad. Or maybe his signature was better disguised. I couldn't really say. Several silent minutes passed. Eventually, David got antsy.

"What's supposed to be happening here?"

"You'll see," Rebecca said.

"That's what I'm afraid of."

"Pipe down. I need to concentrate," I said to both of them. Rebecca snickered, but David grumbled. I knew he was just giving me a hard time, so I smiled and shut my eyes, searching for him again.

Then, all of a sudden, I saw it plain as day. Or maybe I

should say I felt it, heard it? It was hard to describe someone's mental signature. His was different from Rebecca's, in the way that a B is different from a B flat on the chromatic scale. And in the same way I could see music on the page, feel it with my heart, and hear it with my ears, I saw, felt, and heard his signature.

All I had to do was reach out to it.

*Hey,* I thought to him.

*Hey. What are you doing? You're making me nervous.*

*I've created a connection between us that will maintain long distances. At least, that's what I think it will do.*

*Did you do it?* Rebecca asked.

*You can't hear him.* It was a realization, not a question. *And you can't hear me talking to him?*

*Nope.*

*David, can you hear me talking to Rebecca?*

*No, you're also talking to Rebecca?*

Getting tired of the back and forth, I decided to speak out loud. "Okay, it makes sense that you can't hear each other when I'm talking to you separately this way, but why can't you hear me talking to the other person? Once I've found your signature and our connection has been made, shouldn't you be able to hear the thoughts I'm broadcasting all the time?"

Rebecca thought for a moment, and then her face lit up. "Maybe the connections are like highways. You can't drive on both at the same time. So, when you're talking to me, you're on one road that's shared by us. Your communication with David is a separate road, one that I can't hear."

David nodded. "Also, just because you've established a mental connection with someone doesn't mean they have an open door to your head. Consider the way we normally communicate. When I send you a message, you hear what I want you to hear. It makes sense that the rules wouldn't change so dramatically."

I sighed. "It just means it's not perfect, and there's still work to do. If we have a large mission, we'll need to make sure that everyone is not only on the same highway, but in the same car. But we've made progress today," I said, hoping it was enough for now.

David stood to go back to his office, but he stopped and rested his hand on my shoulder. "Good work. Tracy would be proud."

I nodded, not feeling like I could trust my voice in that moment. Rebecca smiled encouragingly at me, her eyes shining with the excitement of our discovery.

He left Rebecca and me alone in the room, and I tried to imagine the real-world applications of this skill. "It might be hard to decide who you need to speak to in a critical moment."

"No, it wouldn't be. I imagine the list of people you'd want to talk to would be pretty short. Me, David, maybe Owen, but that's it." She shrugged her shoulders.

"What about the researchers? Wouldn't it be helpful to be able to tap into what they know without having to call them?"

She paused for a moment, considering the suggestion. "Yes, that would be helpful. You're right. But one of us could always find out what you need pretty quickly if it came down to it. Anyway, we may be overcomplicating it. One step at a time."

"And the next step should be protecting what we've learned. These connections make me nervous." I thought of how easily the Potestas had captured me in Shields' mind. That could happen to any one of us at any time. It would be disastrous if they somehow gained access to our signatures. Without our help, the world would go up in a cloud of Zero. Then a thought occurred to me. Did the Potestas even know the signatures existed? If not, it was all the more reason to keep the information out of their hands.

"It can wait until tomorrow. It's late." She stood and stretched. "I'll see you in the morning."

I nodded, and she left me alone in the training room. I had no idea what time it was, but I wanted to see Owen so I could tell him what I'd learned.

Leaning back in the chair to take a moment of rest before I went to the hospital ward, I shut my eyes and imagined him in his room. I wondered what his signature would be like, and I felt for it, trying to answer my own question.

Perhaps my love for him had taught me his signature long ago, without me even realizing it, because I found it easily. And we weren't even in the same room. I was so excited I nearly lost it.

*Hey, are you awake?*

*What? What the hell?* he asked, a hint of alarm in his internal voice.

*Rebecca and I made some great strides today.*

*Where are you?*

*In the training room.*

*Seriously?* Slowly, his alarm was turning to excitement. *I thought maybe you were just outside the door and didn't want to knock or something.*

*Just wanted to see if I could connect with you from a distance. But there's a lot to do to perfect this method.*

He turned a bit wistful then. *I'll bet.*

*You'll be up and at 'em soon, Owen. You'll see.*

*Sooner than soon actually.* I thought I detected a hint of excitement in his voice, but I couldn't be sure if I was just projecting. *They're releasing me tomorrow.* That was definitely joy I heard, and I loved it, but his news stressed me out.

*What? No!* It was an automatic response, and I instantly regretted it. I knew he would misunderstand me.

*You don't want me to get out of here?* The hurt in his tone was only slightly masked by his confusion.

*No, that's not what I meant. I'm supposed to work with Rebecca tomorrow. I wanted to help you. To show you your...* I hesitated. I hadn't told him about my plan for us to move in together. David had rather reluctantly approved the idea after I'd reminded him that we were both adults—and had been for some time.

I gathered my courage and continued. *To show you our quarters.*

*Our* quarters?

Suddenly, I regretted the distance between us, so I left the training room and started to make my way to the hospital ward. *I thought you might like to share a room. I asked David, and he approved my request...eventually. We have a larger space, two dressers, and a double bed. It's no California king or anything, but it's big enough.*

*One bed?* I could almost hear the wheels turning in his mind.

*One bed.* It was a big step for us. But after what we'd been through...well, I loved him and he loved me, and I wanted to spend my nights with him in every possible way. I knew all too well how short life was. I didn't want to waste it tip-toeing around social niceties.

*I'm on my way to see you. I'll be right there.*

He was silent as I made my way across the facility. My anxiety ratcheted up with each step I made, closing the distance to his room. If I'd assumed too much, moved too quickly, I might have ruined everything. But then again, was our relationship really that fragile? We'd been tested by fire these past months, and we were still there for each other. We'd survived. And we'd survive this, right?

I put one hand on his door, then took a deep breath and went into his room. He had a huge smile on his face, and the sight of his joy filled my own heart with light. "One bed, huh? I think I can handle that."

I ran to his side and flounced on top of him, taking no care for his injuries. He groaned, but he wrapped his lightly bandaged arms around me anyway.

"I need to tell Rebecca I can't train tomorrow, because I'm moving in with my boyfriend."

"Whoa there, you little hussy." His eyes sparkled as he tried to hide his smile.

I swatted his head playfully. "If I'm a hussy, what does that make you?"

His face turned serious. "Lucky."

I laughed out loud and pulled the pillow from behind his head to smack him with it, taking care not to hit his shoulder or arms. "If you think I'm easy, you've got another thing coming."

It was his turn to laugh. "Honey, you are anything but easy."

Things degraded from there until we were both laughing and prodding each other, although Owen was at a serious disadvantage with his bandaged hands.

We lay next to each other in an exhausted heap, staring up at the ceiling with smiles on both our faces. "What time is it?"

"After eleven."

"Rebecca's such a night owl; she's bound to be up."

I tapped into our connection and addressed her quietly, just in case she was sleeping. *You up?*

*Yes. But don't be so whispery. It's creepy.*

I raised the volume of my thoughts a little. *I didn't want to wake you. Owen's moving out of the hospital tomorrow. I can't train.*

*Yay!* The genuine enthusiasm was plain in her thoughts. *What can I do to help?*

*See if you can figure out how to hide your signature. If we're discovered, the signatures could be the Unseen's undoing.*

*Sure. Anything you need.*

*Thanks, Rebecca. Night.*

As I snuggled in next to Owen, I felt content. Yes, terrorists were trying to kill hordes of people with a deadly chemical, but I drew strength from my love for the man next to me.

4

We both groaned when the nurse woke us up in the morning. I was sore from sleeping in such an awkward position, and I knew Owen had to be in even more pain.

"You're going home today, although I see a bit of your home has come to you." She eyed me, but there wasn't disapproval in her look. She seemed to find the situation amusing.

It took most of the morning to get Owen packed up and on his way. He didn't need to sign any release forms or anything like you'd normally do after a long hospital stay, but there was still a lot to gather after such a lengthy stay. It didn't help that he was moving pretty slow. I reminded myself that at least he *was* moving.

Before we left, the nurse reminded him, "Now, you're scheduled for continued therapy four times a week."

He groaned. "Can I have Saturdays off?"

She chuckled at him and shook her head. "It'll be every other day, so sometimes it might be Saturday, sometimes it might be Sunday. But that's half what you're getting now, so quit your whining. Plus, think about the person who has to work weekends to get your butt back into shape. Eventually, you'll go down to three days a week, and you and our nurses can both have your weekends. Just don't be late."

There were three nurses there to see him off, all full-blown members of the Unseen's medical staff. They'd spent plenty of time with him in the last few weeks, and they all seemed like they'd miss him. I wondered what they did when there weren't any patients around. They probably kept inventory, cleaned, and monitored any missions. If the Unseen hated anything, it was being unprepared, and I imagined these nurses were always prepared for the worst.

They offered him a wheelchair to make the transfer, but he declined. He said he needed to walk anyway, and besides, it wasn't that far. We made the trip slower than I would have made it by myself, but not as slow as you'd think considering he'd been in the hospital for the better part of a month. He'd been allowed out of his room for short visits to the living room to watch the occasional movie with us, but nothing more. I could tell from the look on his face that he was really enjoying his freedom.

When I opened the door to our room, I stood back to let him take in our space. The new facility had a lot more space anyway, but our room was even bigger because we were sharing. A couch stood opposite our very own TV, and my keyboard and guitar sat next to the TV stand. Two dressers finished out that wall, and the couch and our bed took up most of the opposite wall. I'd sprinkled some decor around the room, and I'd even found a plant to set between the bed and the couch as a divider. It was fake, but it made the room feel homier. I thought Maddie would have appreciated my effort, if nothing else.

"There's a door. Where does it lead?" Owen asked, looking at the second door in the room.

This was my favorite part of the new facility. The door he was referring to was tucked between the couch and our front door.

"Go see."

Quirking his brow at me, he walked to the door and

opened it, revealing a state-of-the-art bathroom. Granite countertops, glass sinks, and a shower with multiple heads, jets, and temperature settings. The separate tub was a dream. I'd already tested it on several occasions, and I couldn't wait to try it for two.

"We have our own bathroom." He ran his lightly bandaged hand along the vanity as he walked further into the bathroom. "Does everyone have their own?"

"Yup. This facility is awesome. I know you're going to love it once you can explore a little. You should see our view."

"I'm quite enjoying this view." He eyed me, and I could tell what was on his mind. But I didn't think his body was up for what his heart wanted, so I maneuvered him back out into our room. It was worth waiting until we didn't have to worry about aggravating his injuries.

Gently squeezing his hand, I said, "Welcome home, love."

We took it easy for the rest of the day. I helped him get unpacked and settled. He took a nap in the afternoon, and then we had dinner with everyone. They held a huge group meal for him, and everyone chatted him up. We were all excited to have him back, and he was equally enthusiastic about being back.

Even Mitchell spoke up more than usual. "Good to have you topside again." He nodded at his friend between bites of food.

"Someone has to make sure you're staying on task." Owen eyed Mitchell's hand, resting gently on top of Rebecca's, in plain view of everyone at the table.

Camden chimed in. "I think Mitchell has his tasks prioritized just fine without your help, Owen."

There was much hooting and hollering, but Mitchell just smiled. It felt good to see such simple happiness on his face. Rebecca laughed right along with everyone else, and while I thought I detected a faint blush on her cheeks, it could've been a trick of the light. As the conversation devolved into further teasing, neither of them moved to take their hands from the table.

That night, Owen and I climbed into our bed together. He was exhausted after so much activity, so he fell right to sleep, and I snuggled up to him, feeling content as I listened to the soft sound of his breathing. It was an emotion I hadn't experienced in quite a long time.

The next morning, I had to go back to work with Rebecca, so I left Owen to his own devices. He was still asleep when I got up, and I expected he'd sleep well into the morning.

Just to ease my mind, I caught up with Mitchell on my way to the training rooms. He was already mostly done with his workout for the day.

"Can you check on Owen a little later? He was still asleep when I got up."

Sweat pouring off him, he nodded, not willing to pause his workout. Mitchell was a man of few words, but when he said he'd do something, he meant it, so the simple gesture was enough to reassure me.

David stopped me on my way to the training room. I knew that something was wrong before he even said anything, and my suspicion was confirmed when he asked me to follow him into the office.

Once the door was latched behind me, he gestured for me to take a seat. My heart was racing uncontrollably. Had something happened to Owen? Were the Potestas about to strike again?

"There's been word from the Spanish Ministry of Mind Reading. They suspect an attack is in the works, but they're having trouble working out the details."

I sank back in the chair, weighed down by the gravity of what he was telling me. "What can we do?"

"I have Mitchell and his crew working hard to sift through the information sent to us by the foreign ministry. All of our chapters are doing everything they can to get to the bottom of this, but so far, we don't have enough to go on." His brow was furrowed in obvious frustration.

I had no answers, nothing to offer him. But his resolve didn't seem impacted by the uncertainty of the situation. "Keep working. We *will* get to the bottom of this," he said.

"Hopefully sooner rather than later," I said.

As I left his office and made my way to the training room, I felt more pressure than ever to get things right with Rebecca. Time was running out.

Rebecca waited patiently for me in the training room, working on her latest crocheted creation. It was too early to know just what it would be, but it looked like it might end up being a scarf or a shoulder wrap for the cold Colorado temperatures.

"There may be another attack in Spain," I announced as soon as I closed the door behind me.

"I heard." Her tone was low and sad. It felt odd on her, which made me want to fix the problem even more.

With nothing more to be said about it, I asked, "Did you figure out how to hide your signature?" I asked as I settled into the seat across from her, watching her hands work artfully as they pulled the yarn just so.

"Oddly, no. It's almost like a phantom limb for me. Now that I know it's there, I can feel it, but I can't see it. Without being able to see it, I'm not sure how to hide it from intruders." She frowned as she continued to twist and loop the yarn.

"It's a bit of an abstract concept, I guess, just like everything else related to mind reading and defenses. You can't see your thoughts, your memories, the things that make you *you*. But you still have defenses in place, right?"

"But without knowing where my signature is, or even what it is, how can I defend it?" She was clearly frustrated from her lack of progress.

"Maybe I need to do it first, and then I can explain it better."

Sighing, I wondered how much it even mattered. We

needed more than a connection to our peers to defeat the Potestas, find Zero, and stop the killing. It had been days since we'd heard from our headquarters in Washington. They were busy sifting through the possible leads being fed to them by the various branches of the Unseen, like us. David said we'd get news as soon as there was some to give. And the foreign ministries weren't sharing much either. The lack of information, and apparent lack of forward progress, was making me antsy. And there was a new threat in Spain…

"What's up?" she asked, clearly sensing my discouragement.

"I just feel like no matter how hard we work on this, it doesn't matter. We need more weapons to fight them."

"Yes, we do, but we're not going to win the war by rushing it. People all across the country are fighting this. We're going to have a breakthrough soon. It's just a matter of time. Until then, we need to stay focused. It may seem abstract now, but this skill will be immensely useful once we're on the front lines again. You'll see."

"I know you're right." And when the time came, I would be ready. In truth, it would feel good to dispense with all the behind-the-scenes work. I wanted to get into the trenches and stop them before anyone else had to die.

We were silent for a moment, and with nothing else to do but focus on the task at hand, I went back to thinking about our signatures. I wondered what mine looked like. I knew how to detect Rebecca's—and David's and Owen's, for that matter. But my own was still a mystery.

I thought about the things that made me who I was, traveling down the rabbit hole of my internal self for what seemed like an eternity. I watched memories float by, moments, people, and things I held dear, opinions I felt strongly, emotions, and everything else that made up me.

At the end, I found my signature—small, defenseless, and unassuming. It looked to me like a golden treble cleft, giving my life's notes some basic direction.

*Okay, now that I've found you, how do I defend you?* I thought as I held the cleft gently in my hands.

I didn't want to create any defenses that would draw attention to the very thing I wanted to keep secret and safe, but I did want to ensure my safeguards were virtually impenetrable if an intruder found my signature.

I began with a black box. Made of strong, indestructible material of my own imagining, it blended almost seamlessly with the rest of my mind. It had no opening, no hinges, and no lock. The only way to open it was if I placed my own hand on top of it. Once I did, the seam would appear, and the lid would come off. I placed it on the ground of my subconscious, and then let it disappear into the depths of my mind. Someone would only find it if they literally tripped over it, and even then, they'd have a hell of a time getting into it without my permission.

My only concern was that I'd hidden my signature too well. Would this hinder my ability to form connections with the others? But that was a bridge to cross another day.

When I finally opened my eyes, I had no concept of how much time had passed. Rebecca was making notes on the dry erase board in the room.

*Potestas. Zero. Location. Release devices. Timing. Where next? Goals. Defenses. Connections.*

"I think I did it. But I have no idea if my defenses will impede our ability to find each other."

"Oh geez, I didn't even think of that. We'll have more work to do, testing and—"

"All personnel, please report to the conference room at once. Emergency meeting to begin in one minute." David's disembodied voice startled me to attention.

"I didn't know we had a PA system," I said to Rebecca as we rushed out of the room.

"Me neither. Must be special to the new facility?" She hadn't lived in our Florida home for long, but maybe they hadn't had the feature at her old facility either.

Rebecca started following the crowd, but I knew Owen would need help. "Hey, I'll catch up with you later," I said, and she nodded her understanding.

Camden came toward me. He looked like he was coming from the rooms, so I stopped him. "Seen Owen?"

"Nope, just on my way to the conference room," he said in his deep, soothing voice.

"Okay, I'll be right there. I just want to make sure Owen gets to the meeting okay."

Then it occurred to me. *I'm an idiot,* I thought. Why wasn't I reaching out to him through our connection?

*Owen, where are you?*

*I'm coming. Just takes me a little longer is all.*

*I'm nearly to our room. Are you still in there? David said we only had a minute.*

*No, I was in the kitchen getting a snack. I'm nearly there.*

I doubled back and headed for the kitchen, but he was gone by the time I got there.

*Everyone's waiting for you,* Owen said, a hint of satisfaction in his voice.

*Well, if I hadn't been chasing after you, I would've gotten there with Rebecca!*

*Pretty sad you couldn't keep pace with me.*

Biting my tongue as I came into the conference room, I begrudgingly took my seat next to him. I wanted to sit on the other side of the room so I could glare menacingly at him, but those seats were all taken. Once I was seated, David did a head count.

"Good. That went faster than I expected. Next time, maybe we can actually do it in a minute or less." He eyed me, and I looked away sheepishly. The clock on the wall told me I'd delayed everyone by about four minutes.

Without any more preliminaries, David turned on the TV. My stomach dropped as I took in the massive chaos on the screen. The video appeared to have been taken with a camera phone, and it shook, indicating that the person making the recording was running in a crowd of people. It panned around behind, showing what the videographer was running from. The screen zoomed in on bloodied people kneeling in the street, the flesh appearing to melt from their bones. It then panned down to what remained of the videographer's hand, and the phone fell to the ground, the screen going dark.

"No," I breathed. "Spain. We're too late."

"Madrid to be more specific," David answered, not taking his eyes off the screen.

He unmuted the TV when the reporter returned. "Officials fear another attack has occurred. The victims appear to be suffering the effects of Zero, but authorities say it's too early to make any definitive claims. The video you just saw was taken only minutes ago outside the Atocha Railway Station. Hundreds, possibly thousands, of people pass through this thoroughfare on a daily basis. As of now, officials are not speculating on a death toll."

"Why Madrid?" Camden asked.

"Why not? By hitting seemingly random global cities, they're demonstrating that no one is safe," I said, my eyes glued to the screen. Owen reached for my hand and squeezed it, but it did nothing to dissipate the sick feeling in the pit of my stomach.

"But certainly there are places in Madrid that would be more effective if loss of life was their ultimate goal," Camden persisted.

"Agreed. Which is why I don't think that's at the heart of their task. No, they don't mind making sacrifices, but their ultimate goal is power. They want to gain control through fear." I watched as a crowd of people ran screaming from the station. "They're going to get it too."

Owen spoke up, but he didn't release my hand. "What do we know, David?"

"We know that ISIS continues to deny their involvement. And has in fact released a statement that will be given to the media shortly." He paged through some papers in front of him. "We at ISIS do not condone or support the use of the chemical Zero. It is nothing more than a coward's weapon. What can be the gain of such nameless fear? Who attacks this way without explaining their purpose? *Not* ISIS." He cleared his throat when he was finished.

Owen sighed heavily. "By wrongly accusing a known terrorist group, the media may be kicking a hornet's nest."

"Indeed," David said. "But much as it grieves me to say, ISIS isn't our biggest concern right now. It's been just under two weeks since London, and just over a month since Coda. That's three attacks in less than six weeks, with a total death toll of over three thousand people. And that number will climb today, I'm sure."

He paused for a moment to watch the chaos unfolding on the screen. "I think Mackenzie is right. The death toll is remarkably low for attacks of this scale. This is the power play they mentioned."

Normally, I enjoyed being right, but this didn't give me a good feeling.

"The Spanish Ministry has requested reinforcements, so some members of the team based in Washington are flying overseas to help. That means a lot of headquarters' work will fall to us and the other nationwide branches."

He paused, letting us absorb that. "What that means is, we will now be receiving information from Washington to sift through, rather than sending our intel to them. And I'm not afraid to tell you, after this latest attack, it will be a lot. Watch for inconsistencies or anything that seems too obvious. Find any small clues you can to connect the dots between the intel we got before the attack and what actually unfolded. This may help us identify their next move before they make it. We can't make a mistake or a misstep with this one. Lives are at stake. Now is the time for diligence, not fear. I need all of you to double your efforts."

I shot a glance at Rebecca. I hoped she knew exactly

how we were going to do that, because I sure didn't. And Owen seemed utterly lost. At a time when we needed help the most, he was adrift, still trying to make his own recovery from the first attack.

David then turned to Owen. "Owen, now that you're on your feet again, I want you to head up the research team. You'll be responsible for sifting through all the information we get from Washington. You've been with us a great deal of time, so you have a remarkable understanding for how the Potestas operate. You also know firsthand what to expect from an attack made with Zero. You're the clear choice for this post, at least until you're ready to be fully in the field again. I know you won't let me down."

Mitchell nodded to Owen, and a few of the others clapped. Owen's expression remained stoic. I knew he would take his new post seriously, but I could tell he was disappointed about being relegated to research for the time being. But, we were all in the same boat. Information was what we needed, not guns-blazing attacks.

"If no one has any questions for me, let's wrap this meeting up. Stay informed, and immediately let me know of any leads you have."

We all nodded, knowing that went without saying. Slowly, we filed out of the conference room, with noticeably less energy than we'd had going in. There were lives at stake, and I felt like I held every last one of them in my own hands.

# 5

For five days straight, we all worked hard to crack the Potestas' code in the hopes that we would be one step ahead, instead of two steps behind, when we next confronted them. My concerns about the side effect of protecting my signature were thankfully unfounded. I could keep it shrouded from invaders without concealing it from friends. Teaching the skill proved more difficult, but eventually—after what felt like an eternity to both of us—Rebecca finally got it.

Once we had it, we perfected the long-distance connection. However, we decided it would be best to keep the number of connections down to five or less at any one time. Any more voices would be too overwhelming.

Training my peers to create these long-distance connections was challenging in a lot of ways. For one thing, I wasn't used to being the trainer, and patience was not my strong suit. If someone took too long, it was hard for me to continue being encouraging. Luckily for me, my peers were eager to learn our new techniques, but my work with David was awkward to be sure. Really though, what was one more strain on the dynamic between us? Employee, boss; father, daughter; and now trainer, trainee?

We both tried to take it in stride, and he picked up on the technique pretty quickly. The more I worked with him, the more I found his skill to be unlike anyone else's.

"I wish we had more downtime, David," I told him after we were done for the day.

"Why's that?" he asked casually as he prepared to leave the training room.

"Because I'd like to pick your brain."

He laughed and said, "I don't think I'd like that very much!"

"Yes, you would. You could teach me stuff."

"Like what? What do you think I know that you don't?"

"I don't know. That's the point of picking your brain."

He patted my leg. "Soon. I have a feeling all of this will be over soon, and we'll have all kinds of time for picking each other's brains."

That felt ominous, and I didn't say anything as he walked out.

*Meet me in David's office*, Owen said through our connection before I could stew too much about David's comment. The urgency of his tone didn't make me feel any better.

"What? Couldn't get enough of me?" David asked when I followed him into his office.

"Owen said to meet him in here. He's on his way." I could tell he was uneasy, but I was as much in the dark as he was.

Owen didn't keep us waiting long before bursting into the office. "A man has come forward claiming he can save the world from Zero. He's having a press conference right now. It should start any minute."

"What?"

"Here." He turned on the TV and tuned to a random news station. The man at the podium was well dressed, in a full suit and gray tie. His jet-black hair was slicked back, giving him a rather slimy appearance. My intuition

46

immediately told me not to trust him.

"Good evening, members of the press." His voice was clear, deep, and seductive, making me even more leery. "I have come to you today to tell you something special. But first, let me introduce myself. My name is Agusto Masterson. I'm CEO of a lot of companies that will mean nothing to those who are not in the health care industry, and I won't waste your time by listing them. Just know that I can and will follow through on what I'm about to promise you."

He looked up at the crowd and then into the cameras with startlingly green eyes. Paired with his dark hair and pale skin, it made for a striking look. I found myself feeling a bit afraid of him as he looked right through the screen and into my eyes.

"I am going to end the threat of Zero." Cameras flashed in his face, and members of the press barked questions at him, trying to be heard, but he held up his hand to silence them.

"I promise you all, I will answer questions at the end. Just let me get through my speech." Then he chuckled easily, and the audience laughed with him. I narrowed my eyes at the screen. Were they really falling for this guy's sleazy charm?

I wished I could read his mind through the TV screen, but that wasn't really how it worked, at least not yet.

"It appears that Zero is becoming a worldwide issue. The terrorists responsible are using it as a scare tactic to get what they want. They're hiding behind it to create an escalating sense of fear, so that we will be willing to give them whatever they want when they finally do come forward. ISIS has called them cowards, and isn't that rich? I actually think they're geniuses. If they were allowed to continue, unchecked, who wouldn't give them the whole world if they promised to put a stop to their attacks?"

He looked around at the crowd of people who were giving him their rapt attention. He was purposefully using inflammatory language to grab their attention…and it was working.

"But this puts us in a dangerous position. Would we sacrifice our finances, our weapons, our very freedom if it came down to it?" The camera panned out toward the crowd, and I could see some members of the press shaking their heads, others standing stock-still.

"I can't say for sure, but that uncertainty has spurred me into action. I don't like variables. I like known quantities. Waiting to find out what these people are going to do next, hoping that they've had their fun and will leave us alone is too much of a variable. Here's a known quantity for you: I promise you that I will stop those behind Zero for good.

"Due to security measures, I can't tell you *how* I plan to do it, but I can tell you why. I am an extremely selfish person. I care only about my own family. We live in a big city at the heart of this great nation—a likely target, if you ask me. Frankly, I don't want to die. Not yet. Nor do I want any of my family members to be hurt by these lunatics.

"After managing so many different types of people over the years, I've found that selfish motivations are often the most productive. And believe me, this goal *will* be reached. Thank you."

David muted the TV as the press started bombarding the man with questions. "Agusto Masterson rings a bell. Why do I know that name?"

Owen plopped a small file down on David's desk. "This is all we could collect so far, but I've got the team working on it right now. Because he's a big behind-the-scenes CEO, he has his hands in a lot of pots, including oil in the Middle East, tobacco, and health care, as he said."

"What?" I asked, trying to get my head around the apparent conflict of interest. "Health care and tobacco? He makes money off people smoking, and then makes money again when they're dying from it?"

"I suppose so, yes," Owen said.

"Sounds like a real winner."

Owen nodded at my comment, but he seemed distracted. "He has the financial resources to do what he claims. But, at least on paper, he doesn't seem to have the connections he would need. That confuses me. His confidence concerns me. And the Potestas' involvement in this whole mess *really* concerns me. Is this their move?"

"It's impossible to know," David said as he flipped through Agusto's file. "What are his connections to the Potestas?"

"We haven't had time to get that far."

"What do we have to go on, except this gut feeling we all have that he's bad news?"

"Not much. He's very charismatic, and the public and press are eating him up."

"The Bible says the antichrist will be very charismatic. Charisma is not a reason to trust him," I said quietly.

Owen snorted at my comment.

"What? I'm just saying," I said, shrugging my shoulders.

"I don't think he's the antichrist, Mackenzie," David said flatly. "But we need to do some extensive digging. If we manage to find proof he's bad news, we can take him out before this goes any further."

Owen nodded and walked out, leaving David and me alone in his office.

"What do you think?" I asked.

"I don't think it's good, that's for sure." He lowered his voice a few notches, and it left a sinking feeling in the pit of my stomach.

6

That night, while Owen and I were lying in bed, I couldn't stop thinking about Agusto. Owen, however, had other things on his mind. He'd been feeling better and better every day since his release. Now that he was working, contributing again, he was almost back to normal.

He ran a finger along my arm, tracing the length, and slipped it over to my stomach. But the butterflies I felt at his increasingly more intimate touch fluttered away as thoughts of the mysterious CEO continued to plague me. "Agusto is a problem."

His finger paused as he stopped to trace the buttons on the front of my shirt. "You're right; Agusto *is* a problem. A problem for another time." He worked his way slowly up my shirt.

"Maybe." I wanted to focus on him. We hadn't done much more than make out since his release from the hospital ward. It was like a high school relationship, except we had both long since graduated high school. And we still hadn't had sex—first because of my overwhelming grief for Maddie, and then Owen's long recovery process. From the look in his eyes, he had a home run in mind for tonight's game.

Owen slowly unfastened the top two buttons on my shirt. As he worked on the third, I grabbed his hand, startling him. I knew he thought I wanted him to stop, but that was the last thing on my mind.

"You're doing it too slow," I said, looking deep into his chocolate-brown eyes. Then, jumping over the line with both feet, I kissed him hard and we hurtled toward our future together.

Afterward, we lay in bed together, our fingers intertwined, our hands resting on Owen's chest. I didn't feel any regret, embarrassment, guilt, or any of the other dark emotions I'd experienced with previous partners. If possible, I only felt a deeper connection with the man beside me. Our silence was easy, not strained as it sometimes was after the first time with someone new. We fit together, and we both knew it.

But, my paradise didn't last long. Agusto knocked at the door in the back of my mind, nagging me. He was in a *position of power.* Had the Potestas put him there? Did they hope to use him for some massive takeover? But how could they if he really had no connections to them? Something didn't add up.

"We need to know more," I said out loud into the dark bedroom.

Owen rolled over to face me. "I couldn't agree more." The hunger in his eyes gave away his intention.

Playfully, I pushed him away. "I mean about Agusto."

He flopped onto his back and cleared his throat. When he spoke next, his tone was more serious. "Oh. Yes, you're right."

"We need someone on the inside."

"That would be helpful…" He trailed off, not knowing where I was going with this.

But I didn't elaborate. I knew what had to be done. Soon, the rest would know too.

The next day, I requested a meeting with everyone. Once we were all assembled, David gave me the floor.

"What have we been able to learn about Agusto?" I asked.

"Not much. The information is heavily guarded, and what little we've been able to find out is untrustworthy. The same goes for the people around him. His VP is new, but I can't find anything about who they are or where they came from. We know it's a woman, but that's it. Our one reliable source on the inside hasn't been able to get close to her yet. But they are working on it," Owen said. I hadn't told him so, but he was actually quite good at heading up the research team. He seemed to be a born leader, and naturally knew how and where to look for the most important and relevant information to our cause.

"That in itself is suspicious. Don't those big companies usually issue some kind of press release when someone gets promoted? One of my friends just got a promotion and they did this whole write up about him, including his job history within the company. Agusto's hiding something. We need someone on the inside," I said.

David eyed me. "Yes, that would be helpful. But we have no idea how dangerous the situation is. I don't like going in blind."

"I don't think we'll ever know unless we can get our hands dirty. It's best to assume it's going to be dangerous. Hope for the best, plan for the worst, right?" I persisted.

"Who do you have in mind?" he asked, giving me a sidelong stare.

"Me."

For a moment, no one spoke, and then the sound of muted whispering filled the room.

"No. Absolutely not," Owen answered for David, but I could tell from my father's expression that he agreed.

"Hear me out. This is an exciting time for the Unseen. With the long-distance connections Rebecca and I have been working on with you, this could be the fastest and least dangerous way for us to collect the information we need. If we can infiltrate his company and get someone close to him, we could learn directly from the source exactly what he plans to do about Zero, and more importantly, *why*."

"I agree, but it shouldn't be you." Owen remained adamant.

"I'm the one who figured out how to make the connections. If anyone else went, could we rely on them to be able to sever the connection completely? I'm not willing to take that risk the first time our new skill is tested. If they were captured the way I was, it could mean the end of the Unseen." I shook my head. "No. It has to be me."

"So, you admit it's risky." David said it as a statement, not a question.

"Life is risky, David. Does that mean we shouldn't live it?"

He frowned at me, along with most of the other members of the Unseen. Mitchell stayed silent, but Rebecca, more and more frequently at his side, spoke up.

"I agree that planting someone on the inside is a necessary evil. I also agree that it should be Mackenzie." Owen was about to protest, but she cut him off. "However, I do not agree that it is quite as urgent as Mackenzie thinks." She turned to me. "If we gather more information so that we can better arm you, it could save your life and the lives of many others."

"I'm sorry, Rebecca, but I respectfully disagree. I doubt we'll be able to gather any more information in the conventional way than what we already have. His information, if it even exists in digital or hard copy form, is too heavily guarded for us to access it. If we want to know more, we need to get in there. The sooner, the better."

Before Rebecca and I could continue our argument, David said, "Your opinions on the matter are duly noted. For now, I'd like to wait and see what this Agusto's next move is. We can reassess in a few days."

"But—" I started to protest.

"No buts. We wait," he said firmly before he got up and left. The others followed, and Mitchell put a hand on my shoulder as he passed behind me toward the door—a silent gesture of solidarity.

Owen stayed in his seat next to me. I avoided looking at him until the last person had left the room. I thought he'd have a smug expression plastered on his face, but he didn't. He looked just as defeated as I felt.

"What's wrong with you?" I asked, sounding a little more accusing than I intended.

His response was quiet. "It has to be you?"

"It seems that way, yes." I'd stopped asking myself why it had to be that way. It seemed like it just was.

"Maybe this is just my path. And if it is, I have no regrets, because it led me to you." I reached for his hand. He smiled, but the look didn't reach his eyes, which were still clouded with concern.

"It will be okay. I promise."

"You can't promise that!" His sudden change in volume startled me, and he immediately reined himself back in. "I almost lost you once. Why would I ever willingly go through something like that again?" He paused, seeming to consider. "You of all people know what the Potestas can do…and will do. Doesn't that scare you?"

His concern touched me to my very core. It made me want to throw myself into his arms and stay there forever. But our job was to protect people from the Potestas, to put ourselves in the line of danger just like Owen had done at Coda. "Of course it scares me, Owen. I'm human. But, I can't possibly opt out of every dangerous mission. I'd be no use to the Unseen." I paused, thinking how to word my next thought without sounding too arrogant. "You were the one who said we were in this fight for life. And you were right. My exceptional abilities come with certain responsibilities, which is why I think it has to be me. But more than that, I want to help. I *want* to save lives if I can."

He sighed and took my other hand, turning me a little in my chair so we were facing each other. "I love you for it. I just wish you could save those lives from the safety of the research department."

I smiled and leaned in for a kiss. "You just want me to take your place. You hate being stuck in research."

He quietly chuckled. "True enough. I look forward to getting back in the field. And I guess it isn't fair to deprive you of that same privilege."

"No, it's not."

"You are the worst kind of impossible." He stood up and took me with him.

"I've been told that before." We walked out together, and it comforted me to know that we would face whatever lay ahead of us hand in hand.

7

Surprisingly, it didn't take long for us find our next lead.

The next day, Rebecca and I were brainstorming in the training room when Owen poked his head in.

"We have something," he declared, and then instantly walked out. We scrambled to get up and follow him.

By the time we made it out of the training room, David's door was already closing. Mitchell sat next to Rebecca, and they shared a soft look. I glanced at Owen with a half smile, knowing whatever was happening between them was getting serious.

Owen turned on David's TV and connected to the network, going through several layers of security to access a message addressed to him. In order to play the video message once it was open, he had to plug a fingerprint scanner into the monitor and scan his print.

A mousy woman with brown, frizzy hair, steel-rimmed glasses, and a business suit appeared on the screen. "Greetings, fellow members of The Unseen. This message contains highly sensitive information and should not be shared lightly. Your ability to access it will be revoked sixty minutes after it's first opened. We've received word that there's a plot to use Zero against a major metropolitan hospital in the San Francisco area.

"The attack on the UCSF Medical Center is supposedly going to be made within the next forty-eight hours. The San Francisco division believes they can handle it, and they are already investigating. We are waiting anxiously for their update.

"There are several thousand people inside UCSF Medical Center at any given time. This has the potential to be the deadliest attack so far, but because of the details we have in hand, we are confident we can stop the attack before the public learns of the plot.

"We have no leads that might indicate why UCSF Medical Center was chosen, or even why the San Francisco area is a target, but we remain diligent and on our guard, as we expect you all to do. We will keep you updated as more information becomes available."

The screen went back to Owen's inbox, and we sat in silence as we absorbed the information.

Mitchell was surprisingly the first to speak. "How exactly did we come across this information?"

Owen shrugged. "You know what I know."

"It's a bit convenient for my taste," Mitchell said, a frown forming on his face.

Rebecca nodded in agreement. "It feels like a trap. The details haven't been leaked this way before."

"But all other variables follow their pattern. It's a relatively small, self-contained location," Owen answered. "We can't ignore it. Particularly if we can stop it. We have everything we need to do that." He looked to David for confirmation, but he was deep in thought.

Camden attempted to break his concentration. "David, why not wait and see what Agusto does? Maybe it would be an opportunity for him to show us his true intentions. If this guy really wants to be the savior, let him."

He toyed with his mustache, seemingly unaware that we were all looking at him. Owen persisted. "David, you can't really be considering doing nothing. It's the Unseen's job to pursue this kind of stuff."

Silence reigned in the room as we waited for our fearless leader to answer.

"While I appreciate your enthusiasm, Owen, and I don't necessarily agree that we should step back and allow this Agusto character to handle it—although it would be an interesting approach—this isn't our responsibility. As you heard in the message, the division out in San Francisco is handling it. Our job is to continue to find information that will help us get to the bottom of Zero and Agusto."

"But maybe they could use our help," Owen persisted.

I put my hand on his, hoping it would help him settle down. He was so ready to get back into action that he was willing to insert himself where he wasn't needed. Or maybe he thought it would be a good first step, since he would've just provided an extra set of hands rather than taking a more crucial role. I couldn't say for sure. But from the way he instantly jerked his hand from mine, I could tell trying to comfort him had been the wrong move.

"They *can* use our help," David said. "By continuing to find out everything we can. We are of more use to them here, than we would be there."

Owen frowned, and his voice turned cold. "If there's nothing else, I think I'll get back to *helping*." David nodded and Owen walked out, leaving me with my mouth hanging open.

I turned back to David, and he shook his head. "I'm too old for all this angst. All of you need to learn to be team players."

"What can we do for him?" I asked, trying to hide the desperation in my voice. I'd thought Owen was doing so much better, but his outburst had rekindled my concerns.

"Just try to show him the work he's doing is important," Mitchell said.

"In the meantime, the Potestas are barreling down on us, poised to strike at any moment. This plot against the hospital could be a ruse to divert attention from a much larger attack. Has anyone considered that?" I asked, my mind going a mile a minute, as one scenario after another tumbled through it, each more terrible than the last.

"That is a distinct possibility, yes," David said. "But there isn't any intelligence pointing to that, so any contingencies we attempt to put into place would be based on guess work."

"Perhaps some educated guesswork would be better than nothing? What can we do to protect the people we're sending in?" Rebecca asked.

"Nothing really. Our guys are already there. We should know soon who's right." Mitchell said matter-of-factly.

"Excellent," I said flatly. "The more I think about it, the less likely it seems that anything will actually happen to that hospital." I shook my head, trying to banish the image of the sick and injured patients, already bound to their beds, suffering horribly as Zero melted their skin and scorched their eyes and lungs. It was too obvious. Something else was going on, just under the surface, and none of us could put our hands on exactly what it was. Slippery as a fish, the truth stayed just out of reach.

Rebecca and I worked for the rest of the day, which made it easy for me to give Owen some space. But by evening, I couldn't stay away any longer. I found him watching a movie with some of the others.

"Hey," I whispered as I plopped down next to him. He moved just a tiny bit, creating a space between us, and didn't respond. I knew he was upset, but why was he taking it out on me? In that moment, I was very tempted to slip into his mind to find out exactly what was going on there—not only to try to understand, but so I would know how to help him. The damage such a violation of his trust would cause held me back…and left me frustratingly in the dark.

"Can we talk? Somewhere else?" I asked. But he didn't

answer. Instead, he just sat there stoically, watching as Tom Hanks stood at a crossroads in the middle of nowhere. To my mind, *Castaway* had quite possibly the most unsatisfying ending to a movie ever.

"Come on, this is over." I gestured to the TV as I stood up, hoping he would at least acknowledge that I was interacting with him. But he kept staring at it, as if boring into the screen with his eyes would give him some kind of answer about the motivations of Hanks's character, even though the credits were already rolling.

"Fine. I'm going outside to sit by the lake. If you want to join me, that's where I'll be," I said, openly frustrated with him. It wasn't my fault he was in this situation. Maybe I was the one who'd told him there was a plot against Coda, but still. I hadn't been in control of my own body at the time. Besides, there came a point where you just had to accept the things you couldn't change. Que sera sera, and all that crap, right? It occurred to me that I hadn't always felt so zen about life—after all, Maddie's death had undeniably pushed me over the edge—but I buried the thought, hanging on to my frustration.

I stormed outside and slammed the iron outer door behind me, which made a very satisfying clang as it banged shut. The thin layer of snow crunched beneath my feet as I stomped over it. Once I reached the edge of the lake, I plopped down onto a dry rock.

The weather was cold, and I found myself wishing I'd grabbed a coat before I went out. My sweatshirt and jeans weren't going to cut it in the cold mountain air. Christmas was fast approaching. It would be my first without Maddie, but it would also be my first with Owen. Of course, the thought didn't give me much comfort at the moment. With everything that was going on, the thought of celebrating hadn't even crossed my mind. No one had decorated or anything. I was sort of used to that. My guardian Amanda, who'd since joined the Potestas, had resented being assigned to me. Perhaps as a method of revenge, she'd never decorated for Christmas, not even when I was a little kid. But Maddie always did. And as I got older, I started spending the holiday with her family, so I never missed out on the festivities.

As I looked out across the lake, I knew this was shaping up to be the gloomiest Christmas I'd ever had. And Amanda wasn't even around to ruin it for me. Well, she wasn't *here*. She and her new friends were doing plenty to ruin it for us.

I sat out in the cold for as long as I could stand it, hoping he would come. The longer I stayed there, the madder I got, and I started to hope he wouldn't come, for fear I'd say something I'd regret. I'd tried to help him over and over again, and he was ignoring that, ignoring me. Sure, I'd done the same to him when I was grieving, but of the two of us, I'd never been the patient one.

Despite the fact that I'd long since tucked them into my sweatshirt, my fingers were going numb. Just as I was about to turn around and go back inside, I heard footsteps crunching on the path behind me.

Not turning to see who it was—I knew, deep inside—I lifted my chin and stared out at the lake. Owen quietly sat down next to me, but I didn't move over to make room for him. He perched carefully on the edge of the rock, balancing himself with a leg on the ground, while I sat Indian-style, dominating the majority of the space, not willing to give him an inch. Maybe he was making an effort, but damned if I wasn't going to make him work for it.

He draped my coat over my shoulders. "It's cold out here."

Instead of responding, I slipped my arms into the sleeves. It was warm from being inside, and it almost felt like a hug. It made my impatience with him start to dissolve.

"I just want to get back to work. To be useful again." He said it to the lake.

I stared at the moon's reflection in the water for a moment before responding. "Do you remember my very first job? The one where I was asked to research the scientist? Dr. Jeppe?" I drew my knees up to my chin and wrapped my arms around them, holding on to my newfound warmth.

He nodded, and I kept going. "I was absolutely convinced it was busy work. Just something to keep me occupied while Tracy and David figured out what to do with me." I smiled at the memory, thinking about how much my abilities had flustered Tracy. She'd been pretty unflappable other than that. My smile faded as I realized I would never again be able to catch her off guard like that.

"You told me it wasn't, that every job was important. Even the smallest detail could save a life. A nervous tick he had, the place he liked to have his coffee, his favorite newspaper—anything could make a difference, even if it didn't seem important at the time. Come to think of it, that philosophy is probably why you've done so well with the research department."

Chancing a look at him, I saw a smile pulling at the edge of his mouth. "I am pretty smart, huh? Almost wise."

I nudged him with my shoulder and bumped him off our rock. "You're only wise if you heed your own advice."

I made room for him, and he sat down next to me. We both peered out at the lake, so peaceful on this clear night. If the water had been a little more still, we probably could have made out individual stars on its surface. The moon was enough to make it a beautiful picture. It was certainly a far cry from the tropical climate of our Florida home.

Silently, I hoped the peace of the evening would help us both focus on the road ahead. Something big was coming; I could feel it. It hung in the air right in front of my face, just like my icy breath. And I knew it would bring challenges with it that neither of us knew how to face. We would need each other, as well as the rest of the Unseen, before the end.

Narrowing my eyes as I stared out at the lake, I felt ready for what lay ahead. "Bring it on," I said to the darkness, and I felt my words roll through the woods and find their home in the ears of our enemies.

# 8

In the morning, Owen and I were startled awake by an announcement. "All personnel, please come to the conference room at once." It was David's voice, and he sounded...displeased.

"What did we do now?" I asked.

"I don't know, but I'm disconnecting the PA system when the meeting is over. David is abusing it," Owen said groggily. He put the wrong leg into his shorts, and then almost stumbled in his effort to fix his mistake.

When we emerged from our room, it soon became clear we weren't the only ones who'd been awakened by the all call. We looked like a horde of zombies.

"What time is it?" I asked.

"Seven thirty," Owen said through gritted teeth.

We trudged down the hall to the conference room with the rest of the Unseen. David waited for us to take our seats, and we all sort of flounced down, letting our tired bodies sink into our chairs.

"I see most of you weren't too anxious to get to work today," David said, more than a little judgment in his tone.

"David, it's Saturday. Cut us some slack," I whined.

"Agusto has announced a press conference, to air at

eight this morning."

"What is he going to talk about?" I asked, trying desperately to wake up enough to process this information.

"He hasn't said."

"When was the attack on the hospital supposed to be?" I asked, trying to link the two even though I knew it might be reaching.

"Within twenty-four to forty-eight hours of when we got the message. Basically, any time. But we haven't received any updates from the team in San Francisco."

"If the two *are* connected, it'll give us all the more reason to be suspicious of Agusto," I said. The guy gave me a bad feeling I couldn't shake. He was hiding something, and the more public appearances he made, the more certain I was that he couldn't be trusted.

"Let's say it's about Zero or the hospital attack? What can we do?" Rebecca asked.

"It's not overly constructive to speculate. What we can do will depend on what he says. It's unclear whether or not he'll admit to being involved. Maybe he has something totally different to announce. Maybe he's running for president, and this press conference is unrelated to Zero."

*Running for president.* The sentence struck a chord with me. But before I could puzzle it out, David turned the TV on. A few minutes remained before the scheduled start time, but reporters were already covering the conference.

CNN's reporter was a man in his mid-thirties, wearing a black suit and a bold red tie, probably to stand out from all the others when it came time to ask questions. His face was clean-shaven, and his hair was neatly combed to one side, giving him a polished look. "Agusto Masterson, president and CEO of Visco Oil and Agusto Masterson Health Care, has publicly announced a pledge to eliminate the threat of the highly toxic chemical Zero. An unknown terrorist group has used Zero to attack various locations across the globe, putting the entire world on edge as to who will be next.

"Masterson is expected to discuss how he will go about eliminating the threat of Zero. There are many who hope he will even identify who's behind the attacks."

"Does he have that information?" I asked no one in particular.

"I have no idea. If he did, he probably wouldn't release it to the public," David said, not taking his eyes off the screen. "He'd have to explain how he came by it, and if he couldn't, people would probably assume he was involved in some way. He's working hard to gain the trust of the average American. Of the whole world. If he does what he says he will do, we will all be in his debt. It's a scary thought."

Dread settled deep in my stomach, and I reached for Owen's hand as we glued our attention on the screen. In place of the reporter, an empty podium with the occasional bulb flash of a camera appeared on the screen. A low murmur of reporters talking dominated the background noise as I scanned the screen for information.

Owen squeezed my hand, and I loosened my grip, realizing I'd been holding on too tight. The sound of camera's clicking replaced the murmuring as reporters settled into their seats.

Agusto walked out onto the stage, looking much like he did at the last conference. His black suit matched his slicked-back black hair, making him look slimier than ever. He flashed a used-car-salesman smile at the crowd after taking his place at the podium. I held my breath, instinctually feeling whatever he had to say would change our course of action, making our lives—and our work—that much more difficult.

"Good morning, members of the press, distinguished guests, and my fellow Americans," he began. "I've come here to report some good news. But first, let me give you some background information about myself."

"Oh, come on. Just get to it," I breathed, and Owen chuckled.

"My team has been working around the clock to unmask the criminals behind Zero."

"What have we been doing?" I asked, already annoyed with Agusto. He was nothing more than a peacock, if you asked me, one with more money and power than sense.

"It hasn't been easy, and we've sacrificed a lot, but we saved thousands of lives by stopping the enemy's latest plot." Cameras flashed as Agusto displayed a proud smile.

"What do you know about that?" I whispered to David across the table, but he shook his head. Apparently, it was news to him too.

"My researchers were able to uncover a major plot against a San Francisco hospital. A plot that would've resulted in countless lives lost. The terrorists planned to release Zero through the ventilation system. As it rained down on patients and workers alike, it would've ravaged the thousands of people inside the building."

Agusto went on. "A specialized team of government workers were able to use my information to go in and remove the threat before Zero could be released. What's better, we now have samples of Zero to deconstruct, samples that will hopefully tell us more about its makers."

I sat back in my chair, slack-jawed. If he'd gotten a sample of Zero, the plot had to be real after all. But how had he gotten there before our people did? Or maybe the government workers he'd spoke of were the San Francisco division of the Unseen? If that were the case, wouldn't we have been the first to know they'd found a sample? Or that they'd stopped an attack?

David was already dialing a number into the phone in the center of the conference room desk as Agusto continued his monologue. "Thanks to my brilliant team of workers, we've had a major breakthrough that not only saved lives today, but also gave us the tools to possibly save who knows how many lives in the future. We're well on our way to eliminating the threat of Zero, my friends. Thank you."

He paused before speaking again, a small smile on his face. "Make no mistake, we're not out of the woods yet. The attackers are probably not too pleased with me right now. I stopped their plans, saved lives they hoped to destroy." He looked into the camera. "To them, I say: Come at me. We're ready for you." His expression was menacing and unsettling to say the least.

Questions started to pour in. I couldn't tell how he picked a reporter from the bustling crowd, but he pointed at someone, and everyone else quieted down. "Is there anything the average person can do to help?" the reporter asked.

"Of course!" His eyes lit up. It didn't take a mind reader to pick up on the obvious fact that the reporter had been coached. "The most important thing for all of us to do is to be on the lookout for suspicious behavior, and to report anything of that nature to the nearest authority as soon as possible. It was a Good Samaritan's report that brought us to the hospital. She thought she saw someone who didn't belong. She had no proof, no evidence, nothing to back her claim, but we looked into it anyway, and *bam*. Turns out she saved a ton of people. Trust your instincts, folks.

"I've even set up a number you can call with any information you might have regarding Zero or the people behind it. We have people available twenty-four seven to take your calls." A number flashed on the screen, declaring it the ELIMINATE ZERO HOTLINE.

"I've also started a donation fund, called the Eliminate Zero Fund. Although I'm quite wealthy, most of my money is tied up in my companies and private ventures. Anything you can give will help fund our efforts to save you and your loved ones." A website flashed on screen, telling people where to go, and that PayPal was accepted.

Frowning in disgust, I turned my attention back to David. He was speaking quietly on the phone, and had moved to the corner of the room so we could continue to listen to the press conference.

"But if we weren't involved, who was the specialized team Masterson referenced?" he asked. He frowned as he listened to the response. "I understand. Keep me informed. Mmhmm. I'll do the same. Thank you." He hung up the phone, and muted the TV, cutting off any additional questions for Agusto.

"The Unseen were not involved in removing the threat of Zero from the UCSF Medical Center," David declared to the room.

"What? Who was?" I asked.

"We don't know. Apparently, it was Agusto's people."

"What did our people find when they got there?" Owen asked.

"Nothing. No trace of anything. They even checked the ventilation system. Evidently, they posed as maintenance workers so they would have access to all the nooks and crannies in the hospital."

"Smart," I said. Then I remembered what Owen had told us about Coda. "You guys didn't find anything at Coda either, did you?"

"Well, no. But to be fair, we were in more of a survive-and-save-lives mode than a search-and-destroy mode," Owen said.

David's frown accentuated how grim the situation was. "The San Francisco team, whose sole purpose it was to find Zero, found nothing. No canisters, no deployment systems, no trace that Zero had ever been there. They were starting to look at some of the other hospitals and surrounding buildings, just in case the threat had been a diversion, when Agusto announced the press conference."

"When did they go? Maybe Agusto's people had already removed it," I proposed.

Owen walked to the computer in the room that controlled the presentation technology and downloaded a transcript of the conference. He scanned it for any information we might have missed. With his back to the rest of us as he faced the computer screen, he said, "When a reporter asked him when all this went down, he said his people finished cleaning up yesterday."

"But the Unseen were in and out of there all day yesterday. Did they see anyone else?" I asked

"No." David's answer was short, but heavy with meaning.

"Something doesn't add up. If Agusto is lying about dissolving the plot, how did he get samples of Zero to analyze? And why didn't our people see anything?" I asked.

"Maybe it's just a money scheme, you know?" Camden said. "Could be that he's in over his head, and this is how he's getting the public to dig him out. Maybe it has absolutely nothing to do with the Potestas. He's just a money-grubbing slime ball, capitalizing on the public's fear."

We were all silent for a few moments as we considered that option. We spent so much time thinking about the Potestas that it was almost inconceivable they weren't involved, but Camden had probably raised the simplest explanation.

After a time, Mitchell spoke up from the other side of the room. "One lie often leads to another," he said quietly. "Even if he's not just an opportunist, who's to say he really does have samples of Zero? Or, if he does, that he didn't get them directly from the Potestas? *If* he is in bed with them, he'd have access to all the Zero he wanted, wouldn't he?"

A hush fell over the room as we all absorbed the ramifications of what Mitchell was implying.

"I have no answers," David said. Fear flickered across his face before a stony expression took its place.

"We need information, David," I said.

"I agree. We leave tonight for headquarters in DC. Mackenzie, you're going undercover."

# 9

Most of our division stayed behind. David didn't want to abandon our quest for information or our responsibilities to the larger unit, so only six of us—Owen, Rebecca, Mitchell, Camden, David, and I—flew to Washington DC to visit headquarters.

The reason David decided to make the trip with us himself was because he felt like the mission was too important for him to rely on secondhand information. At least, that was how he put it. He seemed to be staying awfully close to me throughout the journey though, which made me feel like I had a little more to do with his decision to accompany us than the importance of the mission.

We landed in DC at about 12:30 AM local time. We were all exhausted, but we weren't done with our day yet. David rented a SUV big enough for all of us, and we drove directly to The Department of Homeland Security. The guard at the gate let us in without any problems after David showed him an ID, making me wonder how many people knew about the Unseen—I mean how many *really* knew. David's badge was just a general ID that apparently gave him permission to be there. It didn't say anything about his security clearance or department.

The brick, rectangular headquarters looked brooding if ever a building could. Windows lined the three bottom floors, with mysterious coverings on the top windows. Honestly, its boxy uniformity reminded me a little of a jail. I wasn't overly comfortable with going inside.

But David didn't hesitate. He parked the car in the virtually empty lot and got out. Whoever we were supposed to be meeting must've parked somewhere else.

We scrambled to file out of the back of the SUV and follow David, but by the time we were out of the vehicle and in the parking lot, he was already at the door, scanning his badge. The door clunked, and he pulled it open as we all rushed forward to join him.

David walked quickly through the lobby, not bothering to turn on any lights, so we didn't get much of a chance to look around. We followed a long hallway, lighted minimally by an occasional florescent bulb in the ceiling. The effect was eerie. All it needed was that creepy hum artificial lighting gave off, and it would feel like we were in some kind of slasher movie.

I rubbed my arms, trying to shake off the willies I'd caught. "This place is creeping me out. Why couldn't we come here during the day?"

"Because they're waiting for us. And our quarters are in here," David responded quietly as he stopped in front of a wall.

We stood around him awkwardly as he stared ahead, seemingly at nothing. I was about to say something when a light flashed in front of him. Apparently, he'd been waiting for the retina scan device to activate. Once that was complete, a panel popped out of the wall to scan his fingerprint. A sharp point jutted out of the scanner to prick his finger.

He jerked back. "Gets me every time."

"What *is* that? Some kind of torture device?" The needle still protruded from the scanner, and the sight of his blood on the tip took the creepiness level up a few notches.

"No, it's a DNA scanner. They prick your finger on the spot, so you can't fake the blood," David said.

Then the wall swung inward, revealing a pleasantly well-lit (much to my relief), stark white corridor. The door closed silently behind us, and we followed David in and continued to trail behind him as he led us through a few turns. Finally, we ended up in a conference room, not dissimilar from our own.

"Seems like we traveled an awfully long way to end up basically right where we started," Camden said, eying the place.

David gestured toward the seats surrounding the white, oval table, and we all sank gratefully into them. After a few minutes, a tall, thin man with tiny, steel-rimmed glasses perched neatly on the end of his nose walked into the room.

"Welcome to headquarters, everyone. I'm Jeffery. I will show you to your quarters."

Somehow, we found the will to stand from our seats, although I was sure a lot of us could've slept right there at the conference table. We followed Jeffery down a few more winding hallways until we reached the rooms that had been reserved for us.

Owen and I shared a nice room that was inviting despite the sterile feeling imparted by the all-white furniture. The bed was very plush and comfortable. Of course, by the time we finally crawled into it, it could've been made of cement and we would've been happy.

I slipped easily into a dreamless sleep, knowing I would need plenty of rest to prepare for the days to come.

We were awakened earlier than we would have liked, but at least it wasn't an all call. Rebecca knocked on the door. "Hey guys, you awake?" she asked in a quiet voice. "David wants a meeting in five."

We groaned, and she must've taken that as a yes, because we didn't hear from her again. We both lay still for a few moments, not wanting to admit it was time to get up. Finally, Owen relented.

"What time is it?"

"Too early." I groaned and rolled back over, covering my head with the plush white comforter.

He met me in my cocoon and kissed my nose. "Time to get up, sleepyhead. Anyway, you don't want to suffocate, do you?"

"If the alternative is getting out of this bed, then yes. I do."

"Your alternative is getting tickled until you fall out of bed." Pinning me beneath him, he brought his hand up near his face and wiggled his fingers. "Make your decision," he said in a dramatic voice.

I sighed heavily, finding it harder to take another breath with Owen on top of me. But I wasn't about to give up so easily. I pushed my hips up into him. "You sure you're so motivated to get out of this bed?"

He eyed me, raising his eyebrows. "That's low," he growled right before lowering his mouth to mine in a savage kiss. I threw my arms around his neck and drew him closer to me, but he only let me enjoy it for a moment or two. "You are a wily minx."

He poked me right in the soft part of my side, right under my ribs, and I squealed. "Fine. I'm up!"

We dressed in record time, but we got lost on the way back to the conference room. I was beginning to despair that we'd be lost in the tunnel-like corridors forever when we stumbled on someone who directed us where to go.

The last to enter, we tried to be quiet and unobtrusive, but as soon as we came in, David drew everyone's attention to me. "Ah, and here she is now."

"Sorry. We got lost." I hung my head as I tried to find a seat. The room was more crowded than it had been the night before. Every seat around the table was full, mostly with unfamiliar faces, so we stood along the back wall with a few others who must've been latecomers. I spotted Jeffery, but he only frowned at me, probably disapproving of my tardiness.

An older man with salt-and-pepper hair, broad shoulders, and a stern expression sat at the head of the table. He didn't look like someone I wanted to cross.

"I hear you're willing to go undercover," he said, his voice low with an edge of gravel to it, like he'd spent too much time yelling at people, or maybe he'd smoked a little.

"Yes."

"There are others who would like to go as well. Today's meeting will cover everything we know about Agusto, and then you six will be given a full tour of the headquarters and our facility here while we decide on the best candidate for the job."

I'd never imagined there would be competition for the job. Maybe there *was* someone better suited. The more time we spent at the headquarters, the more I realized that the Unseen was so much larger than I originally thought. I was having trouble processing it. But there was always a bigger fish in the sea, right?

Perhaps it would be best if someone else were chosen. Owen and David would certainly be happy. But I wasn't sure how I felt about being off the hook. My ego didn't like the idea that someone else would get the chance to stop the Potestas; I had entertained the notion that I was the only one who could stop them for too long to let it go easily.

Before I could bristle too much, the stern man continued talking. "My name is Davis. I'm a former colonel in the military, so I will not waste time sugarcoating this situation for you. Whoever takes this job will be diving headfirst into enemy trenches.

"Agusto is suspected to be a high-ranking member of the Potestas. His financial status, the guards that travel with him at all times, and the fact that there's very little personal information on him available all point to that fact. We're just not sure how high."

It felt like I'd been punched in the gut. I thought about how Amanda's history had been erased after she joined the Potestas, and suddenly our lack of information on Agusto made sense.

"Because of his suspected status, I want you all to understand how dangerous this mission will be. The man you're going to follow could be third or even second in command. You will be deep into enemy territory, and you will be alone. The risk is high; the probability of success is low. It's important for you understand that before you proceed.

"Although we have nothing specific on Agusto, men of his caliber are known to swiftly eliminate those who get in their way. In fact, he's been seen associating with several known contract killers. So, tread lightly.

"It will be your job to gain his trust, find out what we need to know, and not get killed. Get in, learn as much as you can, and get out. Nothing more, nothing less.

"Now, knowing the risks involved, I want those who are still willing to volunteer to raise your hands. You will not be judged if you decide to stay behind. You will be put to work here. There is much to do to both prepare for this mission and see it through to success. Each of you must play your role to the absolute best of your abilities, or we are sure to fail. The agent who goes undercover is just a small part of this." He paused, taking a moment to look at each of the faces in the room. I wondered what assessment he was making about me as he stared me down with cold, blue-gray eyes. I shifted in my seat nervously before he moved on to the next person.

"Do I have any volunteers?" Six hands went up in the end. Two from our ranks—Owen, me, and four others I didn't recognize. Disapproval clouded my gaze as I looked at Owen's outstretched arm. He shrugged, and I shook my head no at him.

"If you think I'm going to let you head right into the snake pit again without a fight, you can think again," he whispered.

"If you think I'm going to let *you* throw yourself into that same pit before you're ready, you're dumber than you look." He nudged me with his elbow, but I didn't smile. This was serious business.

"Okay. Thank you for your willingness to be on the front line of this fight," Davis said. "The chosen candidate will be announced tonight. Meet back here at five o'clock for our decision." He looked straight at me, and I gave him a terse nod before flying out of my seat, suddenly eager to escape the room. I couldn't put my finger on why he made me so nervous; I just knew he wasn't someone I wanted to disappoint.

David met us out in the hall. We would take a tour of the headquarters while the leaders deliberated on which one of the volunteers to send undercover. "I'm staying here to help. Besides, I've seen this place before. You guys go, have fun." He put a hand on my shoulder, and I wasn't sure how I felt about his involvement in the vote. I was sure he'd vote against me, and the realization made me angry.

"David, don't you think you're a bit too biased to be on the selection committee for this particular mission?" I didn't want him to choose Owen over me, and I really didn't want the slap in the face of him choosing a stranger over his own daughter.

He looked at the rest of our tour group, which included Jeffery, who would apparently be our guide. "Why don't you guys go ahead? She'll catch up in a second."

Owen hesitated, but I nodded for him to continue onward. I didn't want him to try to argue his case with David. I could tell he didn't want to listen, so I was grateful when he fell into step with Mitchell and Rebecca.

It was all the prompting Jeffrey needed to start the

tour. The cadence to his voice reminded me a lot of C3PO. That, combined with his gawky stature, really made him resemble the likably annoying robot. I made a note to share my observation with Owen later—it was sure to give him a laugh given his obsession with Star Wars. Of course, Owen wasn't my favorite person at the moment, so maybe I'd save that little tidbit for later.

"Listen, it's no secret that I don't want you to go on this mission. But I also know you're the most well-equipped member of the Unseen for the job. You're right; it will be a difficult choice, and I won't make it lightly."

I had only been with the Unseen for a few months. Doubt started to creep into my thoughts again. How could I possibly be the best person for the job? "What do you know about the other volunteers?" I asked, not sure I wanted to know the answer.

"Well, I know Owen sure isn't ready for this yet." His comment made me laugh, but it was more of a stress release than anything else.

"And I know the others are very skilled," he finally said. "Two are some of the highest-ranking trainers among the Unseen. More skilled even than Tracy."

*What could we learn from them?* I wondered.

"It will be a tough choice," he repeated.

"Just promise me something." I paused, not surprised when he waited for me to continue before making any hasty guarantees. "Don't make your choice based solely on your desire to keep your daughter safe."

A few more moments passed before he responded. "A choice like that is one I would never regret, Mackenzie," he said. "Even if you'd hate me for it." I had no idea how to respond to that. Once again, he'd blurred the lines between boss and employee, father and daughter. So, I simply nodded and rushed down the hall in the direction the tour group had gone, suddenly eager to escape the intensity of our conversation.

The group hadn't made much progress while David and I were chatting, so I caught up with them easily. Once I rejoined them, I looked back, but David was already gone. Owen was standing with Mitchell, and I deliberately stood next to Rebecca instead of him. Childish? Yes. But I had too much on my mind to worry about my maturity—or lack thereof.

Jeffery had stopped in front of what appeared to be a workroom, but it was significantly more sophisticated than anything in our new facility, let alone our old one. I felt like I would need years of training just to operate the technology in the room. I couldn't even begin to guess what all of it was for. Luckily for me, Jeffery gave us a brief summary before moving on.

"Our workrooms are equipped with the latest scanners, servers, surveillance, and informational devices. If the information is out there, we are equipped to find it."

I thought about Agusto as we walked to the next stop on the tour. All that technology hadn't revealed too much about him. There was still something to be said for manpower, which was a surprisingly comforting thought. In the face of such impressive technology, I was still needed.

After a few more stops on the tour, we ended at the cafeteria. It was huge, which gave us an idea of just how many people worked at headquarters.

Even though it was lunchtime when we arrived, there weren't more than twenty people in the cafeteria. "Where is everyone?" I asked Jeffery.

"We all take our lunch at different times. That way we don't overwhelm the cook. Anyway, about fifteen percent of our employees aren't even on duty yet. Someone is always working, even at night."

"Seemed pretty dead in here last night," I said, half under my breath.

"Yes, well, as you've seen, our facility is large," Jeffrey said. "It's easy to be, well, unseen here."

Nodding, I snickered at his pun.

"Enough talk. What's for lunch?" Camden asked. Jeffery gestured toward the line, and we all followed him and grabbed what we wanted from the display. They had a good variety of food ranging from sandwiches to pasta salad, all different kinds of fruits, and a variety of chips and snack items.

Once the six of us were seated with our lunches, Jeffery excused himself.

"Wait, what do we do after this?" I asked around a mouthful of pasta. I hadn't expected him to just leave us.

"Whatever you like, I suppose. I was given no instructions beyond 'give them the tour.'" He shrugged and walked away.

"Does he remind anyone else of C3PO? Even the way he acts is a bit robotic," I said in an undertone after he was out of hearing range.

Mitchell responded right away. "Thank you. I've been trying to place him all morning."

Owen smiled, and it was all I needed to accept peace with him. He was just trying to protect me after all, and I him.

"What should we do until tonight's meeting?" I asked as I stuffed more food into my mouth. I hadn't realized how hungry I was until I started eating.

Owen looked at me slyly. "I can think of a few things."

I nudged him, and Camden cleared his throat. Rebecca yawned. "I don't know about the rest of you, but I could go for a nap."

Mitchell perked up, and the look the two of them shared was unmistakable. "Not sure how much sleeping you're going to do," I said, unable to stop myself.

After he turned three shades of red, Rebecca came to the rescue. "I meant I wanted to actually sleep, thank you very much. After the early wake-up call and late night, I'm exhausted."

"I don't know if I can sleep. I need to move. Do something productive," I said, and Camden nodded. He seemed relieved to have someone on his side, since he was the only single guy with us at that moment.

"You can totally go do something productive if you want, Mac. I'm going to get some Zs. I feel like a zombie." Rebecca stood with her plate.

"Okay, well, you can find me in one of the workrooms later if you want. Otherwise, I'll see you at tonight's meeting."

"Sounds great," she said and walked away. Mitchell stood without comment, and after giving us a smile and a shrug, he followed her.

"Can you blame him?" Owen asked.

"Nope. I'm glad they're happy," I said as I watched them walk away. Rebecca reached back for Mitchell's hand without turning to find him. He connected with her naturally, and they fell into step. "They fit together." Opposites really did attract, and when they did, it was magical.

Owen nodded as he finished up his lunch. "I think I'll go lay down for a bit too. The idea is too enticing. Sorry, Mac."

"No, you need to rest. Come find me when you're ready. What about you, Camden?"

Camden nodded. "I'm in. Let's find something to do."

"Great." Owen kissed me lightly before he left, and Camden and I made our way to a workroom. There were computers and monitors everywhere, with people working busily at each station. We both selected a computer and sat down.

I stared at the screen for a few moments, not sure what to look for, knowing all the workers around me were certainly researching Agusto, his company, and what I'd be getting myself into if I was chosen as the plant. Then his disgusting fund popped into my head. I wondered how much money he'd already raised for his cause, and if there was any way of telling how much—if any of it—was actually going to stop Zero.

I typed in THE ELIMINATE ZERO FUND, and the website popped right up. After clicking over to it, I learned in big, red letters that they'd already raised a million dollars in the twenty-four hours since funding had started. David was right. If Agusto did succeed, people would blindly give him whatever he wanted. It was a dangerous thought, for someone who was such a question mark.

I spent the rest of the afternoon trying to find the name of the bank where the money was being sent, but I had no luck. "If it's out there, we have the resources to find it, huh?" I asked the computer, just as Owen put his hand on my shoulder.

Relaxing at his touch, I rested my hand on top of his. "How'd you sleep?"

"Like a log. Glad I set an alarm. It's time to go to the meeting and find out who they've chosen."

"Already? It seems like I just sat down." Suddenly, a gamut of emotions washed over me. Stress, excitement, and anxiety all warred for space in my head.

My mouth went dry as Owen took my hand and led me down the hall to the conference room. I looked back at Camden, and he gave me two thumbs-up and a goofy smile as he followed us.

We took our seats and anxiously awaited the arrival of the committee. The sounds of people shifting in their chairs, clearing their throats, and smoothing their clothing dominated the room. No one had the nerve to speak, not even those who hadn't volunteered. The tension in the room was taut enough to keep everyone's mouths shut.

Finally, Davis came in with David and two others. They took their seats at one end of the table. David looked tired and embattled, his eyes a bit sunken, his hair sticking out in directions it didn't usually go. He'd fought hard for this decision. Had he won?

"We've deliberated for hours over this choice," Davis

said. "This is quite possibly one of the most important missions the Unseen have ever undertaken. We haven't made our decision lightly.

"Some of you have years of experience and a long list of extensive skills you alone have mastered." He turned his gaze to me. "Others have a natural ability the rest can only dream of." I shifted in my seat.

"Please know that just because you weren't chosen, it doesn't mean we felt you were unsuited for the task. We've made the selection we feel will give our team the best odds for success. If we thought you would be more useful behind the scenes, you were eliminated from the running. Nothing more, nothing less."

I glanced at Owen, whose face revealed no emotion whatsoever, but his grip on my hand remained tight.

"That being said, the candidate we've chosen to go undercover for the Unseen to investigate Agusto Masterson is Mackenzie Day."

The room let out a collective breath, but I still held mine. I understood that I was to be the one to stop the Potestas, but it was in that abstract sense we all know we were going to die someday. It seemed so far off. Now, it was real, staring me in the face, and all I wanted to do in that moment was plant my hands on its shoulders and push back.

Instead, I took a deep breath and nodded to Davis. I couldn't look at Owen or David, whose expressions would be full of heartbreak, concern, or some other emotion I couldn't process at the moment. No, I stared right at Davis, trying to show him I was strong enough and worthy of the cause.

Owen squeezed my hand a little tighter, but I wasn't sure if he was encouraging me, or trying to hold on to me.

Davis nodded briefly to me, and then moved on. "The rest of you will be given your assignments individually. Those of you from Mackenzie's group will stay here on location until the mission is complete. I hope you all know you're in for a long haul. This won't be easy for anyone."

Turning to address me specifically, he said, "Mackenzie, your transformation starts first thing tomorrow morning."

# 10

That night, Owen and I lay awake in bed, unspoken words hanging heavy in the air between us. We both stared up at the ceiling, trying to comprehend our future—and if we would still have one after all this was over.

As the minutes stretched on, I started to get worried that this was how we were spending our night together. Then I got irritated. I didn't want to admit out loud that it might be one of our last nights together, but I wanted it to be special.

Throwing caution to the wind, I rolled on top of him and kissed him with all the passion I felt for him, for the Unseen, for doing what was right, and for saving lives. I let it all flow through me, and he responded in kind.

No, we didn't sleep that night, but at least we didn't spend our time staring up at the ceiling, wondering, worrying, and afraid.

I was too keyed up in the morning to be exhausted. Davis hadn't elaborated on what my "transformation" would entail, so I had no idea what to expect.

David met me outside my room promptly at eight. Before I went out to meet him, I shared one last moment with Owen. "I love you."

He nodded as his dark eyes sparkled in that way that turned my insides to mush, and I didn't need to hear him repeat the words to know he felt the same way. I'd never said it to anyone except Maddie before, but my inexperience didn't make it any less true.

David led me down the hall to an unfamiliar room. "Jeffery didn't show us this room. What is it?"

"It's where you'll become Agusto's assistant," David answered.

"Agusto's assistant? How did you manage that?" I asked, excited and nervous at the same time. This meant I would be much closer to Agusto than I would have imagined possible.

"We haven't managed anything yet. You still have to get the job. All we've gotten you is an interview with Agusto."

I swallowed hard. "So if I don't get the job, the mission is done before it can even get started."

"You better make a good first impression then," David said as he held the door open to what I mentally dubbed the transformation room, and a team of people met me on the other side.

First was hair. They cut it short and dyed it platinum blonde. It was pretty trendy, but the difference was shocking to me. My hair was a tangled mess most of the time, but the pixie cut didn't suit me. It made the angles of my face too prominent.

David stood behind me as I gazed at myself in the mirror, and he must have gleaned my thoughts without reading them, because he asked, "What's wrong?"

"It…it isn't me."

"That's kind of the point, Mackenzie."

Frowning, I nodded. What else were they going to do to me?

Next, I was fitted for color contacts. They gave me explicit instructions for how to put them in, take them out, and care for them. Once I was on the inside, there would be no physical contact with the Unseen, so I had to make the pairs I was given last. They offered me two pairs, but I asked for three in case I lost one. I wasn't used to wearing contacts at all, and they burned at first, but I was assured I would get used to them.

"I don't like Agusto. How am I supposed to make a good impression?" I asked as the transformation specialists were pulling something that looked rubbery out of a mold.

"You don't have to like him. You just have to get him to like you. Turn on the charm. And for God's sake, keep the snark to yourself."

I lowered my voice while the other members of the team were still a few feet away with their rubbery creation. "Are you sure I'm the best person for this job? I'm excited, but I'm also a little nervous. Are you worried?"

"No matter what the mission, no matter who's sent as our undercover agent, we are always worried," he said as they approached with the rubber. It was a prosthetic nose. They showed me how to apply it, and then let me practice doing my makeup around it. They also advised me on how to make my makeup heavier and darker than usual. In the end, it didn't look bad, just different.

When they were done, I stood in front of a full-length mirror and examined the effect. I was dressed in a navy pinstripe suit with a baby-blue blouse underneath, modest navy-blue heels, my hair gelled into messy-on-purpose spikes, and a trendy little headband to hold back my bangs. Dark blue dangly earrings and a matching necklace completed the look. They'd changed my brown eyes to a soft sky-blue, with flecks of dark blue in them that complimented the blues in my outfit. The person staring back at me was startlingly attractive. But, at the same time, she made me uncomfortable. I'd already spent time looking at the world through someone else's eyes. I wasn't thrilled I would be doing it again.

David walked up behind me with a file in hand. "This

information details your work history, your qualifications for the position, and the background of Joyce Nye. The team worked hard to create this person, and to make all of her credentials valid, should Agusto want to check up on you. Study it like it's your gospel. That is your life story. Believe it, and you might just get the job." The glint in his eye told me he was teasing me, but I couldn't smile back at him. It was all a little overwhelming.

"You okay?"

"I guess so. It just feels odd to be sort of trapped in someone else's skin so soon."

He took opened his mouth to speak, but then shut it without saying anything. "I hadn't thought of it that way," he finally said.

We stared at the girl in the mirror for a few minutes. I wondered if she was strong enough for the task at hand.

"So, did the vote go your way?"

David gave me a soft smile. "I wondered how long you'd wait to ask me that. Let's just say, I think the decision we made will give us the best possible outcome for success."

"That's not an answer," I said, not wanting to let him off the hook so easily.

He shook his head, a slight hint of sadness in his eyes as he put a hand on my shoulder. "The father in me is…worried, to say the least."

Tilting my head, I gave his reflection a half smile. "I promise to touch base with you every night through our mind-reading connection." I chuckled. "Because that's not weird at all."

The sadness drained from his face, replaced with a genuine but reserved smile. "Yes, well, you're surrounded by weirdos now. And hopefully, those weirdos will keep you alive."

"Hopefully." I whispered it to the girl standing in front of me.

As I stared at her, I thought about the way I'd felt

going into our last mission, the one that had ended with my imprisonment inside Dylan Shields. I'd been at once excited and scared, particularly after we learned what we were getting into. This time, the nerves were there, but they felt more like jitters than real fear. A calm swept over me, brought on the wings of my newfound confidence. I was confident I was capable of tackling this mission, and some pretty high-up members of the Unseen thought so too.

*We've got this,* I thought as I stared at the unfamiliar face in the mirror, and she nodded back at me.

Before the team showed me how to get everything off without ruining it, they let Owen come in and see the disguise. He didn't recognize me. He stood like a lost puppy near the team of people who'd worked on me.

"Owen, it's me," I said cautiously as I walked toward him from the middle of the group. I had no idea how he would react to this look, and he'd been somewhat unstable lately. The last thing I wanted was for him to turn away from me now, before I went undercover.

He did a double take and then stared at me with wide eyes as the team dispersed to give us some time alone.

Holding my arms out for his inspection, I shrugged. "What do you think?"

"I don't know." I could tell from his tone he was being totally honest.

"I don't like it," I admitted, hoping that would be an icebreaker.

"Why not?" he said as he stepped closer, appraising the girl in front of him as he went.

"It's not me. I'm looking at the world through someone else's eyes. Again."

He reached out for me with a pained expression on his face that quickly turned into the mischievous look I loved. "I don't know," he said as he took my hands. "I think she's kind of hot."

I scoffed and jerked away. "You *would* like her." He took me in his arms, and I playfully tried to push him away. "She wears too much makeup."

He honked my fake nose. "And her nose is a bit hollow."

Davis walked up, so we separated, stifling our laughter.

"Mackenzie." He held out a purse to me. It was a bit comical to see such a stiff, former military man holding a purse out at arm's length, but Davis wasn't the kind of man you could laugh at.

"Inside, you'll find your new driver's license, various credit cards in your name, some cash, and anything else you might need for this venture. You won't be staying here at the facility during this mission, so you'll also find keys to your apartment. You need to have a legitimate residence in case you're followed. This is the address." He handed me a piece of paper. "It's within walking distance of Agusto's office. I think you'll be doing a lot of walking, so I hope those shoes are comfortable."

They dug into my ankles as if to tease me. Maybe I just needed to break them in.

"You're to report to Agusto's office first thing in the morning, so this will be your last night with us until the mission is either aborted or completed. Before you go, you need to be certain you understand how to apply your disguise without our aid. Please take advantage of the team while you have them.

"As you know, one of our members has already been implanted within Agusto's company. She's been able to tell us that Agusto is heavily guarded at all times, which is why it was vital to get you a position so close to him. Obviously, being that close is not without risks, but we need to know what he knows, what his motivations are, and who he is."

I nodded and peeked into the purse. My new driver's license had a picture of the new me, taken no more than an hour ago. Seeing a different name next to a picture of the new me was a lot to take in.

*You'll help me along the way, right?* I thought to Owen.

*Of course, Joyce. You know, I like dating two women. It's exciting.*

I returned his smile with a glare, but Davis was still in front of us, so neither of us did any more.

"David told us about your talent for communicating over long distances, which we think will aid this mission's success tremendously. Keep us as informed as possible. Any tiny detail you manage to uncover could be the key to unlocking the source for Zero, where the Potestas plan to attack next, or who Agusto really is."

"Of course, we're assuming I'll get past the interview," I said, unsure of how I felt about facing such high stakes right out of the gate. Davis only stared at me in response, as if what I'd said didn't deserve any kind of acknowledgement. Of course I would get past the interview. Why would I even say something like that?

*Good thing all they want me to do is save the world.*

*You've got this*, Owen thought back to me.

I could only assure myself he was right. There was no other option.

There was only one last detail to master before I left for my—or, rather, Joyce's—interview in the morning—how I would stay hidden from Agusto's security.

My transformation had been exhausting, but I knew my time undercover would be over before it began if I didn't learn how to protect myself, so I doubled down to listen to Davis's explanation.

"Our mole in Agusto's company tells us that each new employee goes through basic mind screenings. If the subject is not a reader, he or she won't even notice, but you will. You'll need to hide your defenses. Of course, you'll still need to let stray thoughts out to reinforce the impression that you're not a reader, but this goes beyond that."

"But what if I'm legitimately attacked?" I asked, not comfortable with the thought of burying my defenses.

"The cloak doesn't work for attacks, only probes. If someone goes in with the intent to muck around, your defenses will activate." He pulled up a chair, and one of the transformation crewmembers brought me one too, so we could sit down facing each other.

"It's almost like placing a giant, black cloth over your whole mind," he said, trying to explain the abstract concept to me. "Give it a go."

I shut my eyes and visualized a huge cloak coming down over everything, my defenses, my memories, my subconscious, everything. I didn't know what was supposed to happen once it had settled into place, but I didn't feel any different. Opening my eyes, I shrugged at Davis.

"Now what?"

"Now I see if your cloak is effective." He shut his eyes, and I sat uncomfortably as one of the highest-ranking members of the Unseen tried to probe my head. It felt like a light push on the outskirts of my mind, and it was unsettling to say the least.

After only a few moments, he opened his eyes again and smiled. "Good. Just make sure you study Joyce's file to the fullest. You need to place some of her memories outside the cloak, so they find something when they probe you. If you're not a reader, they'd be bombarded with the things that make up Joyce. You need to put those things into place."

"Sure," I said, even though I was anything but sure.

He nodded succinctly at me. "You'll be ready. Try to get some rest, and we'll see you in the morning."

I nodded at his instruction, but somehow, I didn't think I'd be getting much rest at all.

That night, after spending hours absorbed in memorizing all things Joyce Nye, I showered and took off the removable portions of my disguise, then slipped into bed and laid my head on Owen's chest. He ran his hand through my closely cropped, now-blonde hair. "I kind of like it. It's soft."

"Like petting a dog or something?" I teased.

He laughed. "Maybe. But at least you don't smell like one."

"Yes, that is a plus."

We were quiet for a few moments as I played connect the dots with the freckles on his chest. He didn't have many, so it made for a short game, but it kept my hands occupied while I thought about the coming days. After not sleeping the night before, I should've been exhausted, but my mind wouldn't turn off.

"I don't think I have to tell you that I'm not thrilled about this, Mac."

"I know."

"Just don't do anything stupid, like getting yourself turned into a robot. Oh wait…"

I swatted him, and he laughed.

"Seriously though. Come back to me."

"I will," I said.

One way or another, I knew it was true.

# 11

Long before the sun came up, Owen and I said our quiet goodbyes. He wanted to say goodbye to me, not Joyce Nye, despite the fact that he planned to stay with me for most of the morning. The conversation was silent, carried on through tender looks and gentle touches. We'd said everything that needed to be said the night before. All that was left was to move forward.

He walked me to the transformation room, where I worked as quickly as I could to become my alter ego.

The team had a few minor tweaks to make, but overall, they were impressed by my performance. It took me over an hour to get everything just right, and I knew that would have to be factored in to my daily routine. I wasn't used to spending so much time on myself. Normally, I liked to sleep as long as possible and walk out the door looking one step above awake. But this mission called for more than that.

Owen waited for me near the entrance of the transformation room. This time, he recognized me as soon as I approached him. "Joyce," he said. "Where shall we tell our better halves we are this time?"

I swatted him, and he laughed as we walked to David's

makeshift office, which was really his quarters, spruced up with a laptop, portable file folder, and a giant monitor hanging on the wall that the rest of us didn't have.

I knocked quietly, not wanting to wake him up. Even though I'd been up for almost two hours, it was still before sunrise. "Come in, Mackenzie."

"Not Mackenzie. Joyce," I said, closing the door quietly behind me, knowing Owen would wait for me on the other side, like he always did.

David sat on his bed, dressed in sweatpants and a T-shirt, his computer on his lap. Of course I hadn't woken him up. That would require him to stop working long enough to actually sleep. "Ah yes. You've done a good job learning how to apply all this." He gestured vaguely at my overall appearance.

"Thanks." I wasn't sure if it was the compliment or the attention to the new me that made me uncomfortable, but I changed the subject. "Well, I'm off. I just wanted to say goodbye."

"How are you feeling?"

"Actually, I feel pretty good. Don't get me wrong, I'm terrified of the interview, jittery, and I know I'm bound to mess up about half a million times, but we'll get through this. I know it."

"Just don't sass him, and you'll do fine. I'm very proud of you, Mackenzie."

"Thanks?" I phrased it like a question, not sure how to respond to such emotion from my boss. Yes, he was my father, but we didn't usually do the father-daughter thing.

"You were born to do this. I have every confidence in you."

In that moment, I knew he was right. I walked over to the bed, and we shook hands. It felt more natural than a hug. He turned our hands over, putting his other hand on top of mine.

"I *know* you won't disappoint me," he said, and I tensed up at the word, even though his tone was soft. "I know that because I've realized nothing you could do would disappoint me."

Smiling, I wondered about the man sitting before me, and what our lives could've been like if we'd spent them together.

"We'll talk soon," I said as I let go of his hands—only then realizing how much warmth they'd imparted.

When I got to the door, he quietly said, "Good luck."

I turned around in the doorway. "Thanks, Da—" But I still couldn't do it. It felt too foreign on my tongue after all those years alone. "Thanks, David."

Acting like he hadn't noticed, he smiled warmly at me as I walked out.

By the time I met Owen in the hall, Rebecca was waiting with him.

"Hey stranger," she said. I hadn't had a chance to see her the night before, so this was her first introduction to Joyce.

"What do you think?" I asked and did a little twirl in the hallway.

"It sure is different. But you wouldn't look unusual if I didn't know how different this is for you. In fact, she's quite striking."

The three of us started walking out of the building together. "Well, I hope that's a good thing," I said, suddenly nervous about the mission as I got closer and closer to leaving my family behind. "I mean, do I want to be that noticeable? Memorable? Don't I want to blend in?"

"In the high-powered business world, well-put-together women are a dime a dozen. You'll be fine. So what's your plan of attack? You have to absolutely nail this interview. I know we're all hoping he'll just give you the job on the spot, but that's unlikely. Try to be calm and patient," Rebecca said, getting right to the heart of things.

"What if I don't get the job?" I asked.

Rebecca hesitated as we walked, and then shrugged. "Well, you're sort of a chameleon. I suppose we can just bring you back here and remake you, then toss you back into the ring."

Her response made me stand up a little taller. She was right. We were more resilient than that. If he passed on me, we'd find another way in. It was what we did. It would work out either way.

Mitchell was waiting outside the main entrance, taking in the sunrise. I nodded to him, and he nodded back. "Have a sundae for me, okay?"

"I will," he said, smiling at my mention of our code.

Owen stopped walking then, and our arms were pulled tight when I kept going.

"I'm going to stay here with Mitchell," he said.

"I'll just go tell the cabby you're coming," Rebecca said. "Mitchell?"

He nodded and walked on.

"She's subtle, isn't she?" Owen said, a small smile on his face. I tried to burn it into my memory since I wouldn't get to see it again for a while if I was successful.

"You know I love you, right?" he asked.

"Impossibly."

He smiled and lifted his hand to my face, stroking my cheek with his thumb. "You are the worst kind of impossible."

I leaned in to kiss him. It was soft and full of meaning. "So I've been told." Taking a step back, I held on to his hand as I started to create distance between us.

"Don't do anything stupid," we said at the same time. We laughed, and that was how I left, with laughter. I wouldn't have it any other way.

I passed Mitchell, who gave me one last nod, and joined Rebecca at the curb. The cab had already pulled up to give me a ride to my new life.

She smiled knowingly at me, clearly understanding how hard it was to say goodbye. "Just make sure you remember to let out stray thoughts while you're undercover. Just because you have that fancy cloak in place doesn't mean you can be careless. He's probably high ranking and highly skilled. Stay focused on what he wants you to do, and do it right, so he doesn't notice anything odd about you. And don't get frustrated if it takes some time. Learn to do the job he wants you to do first so you can gain his trust and confidence. Then start digging. Don't worry about any of this until you're past the interview, but I assume you'll knock that out of the park. I mean, who wouldn't love you?"

As she rattled off my responsibilities, I nodded along, laughing all the while. "Okay, Mom."

She leaned in and hugged me. "Above all, don't do anything stupid."

I pulled away and gave her a mock hurt look. "Why do people keep saying that to me?"

Her expression turned serious. "Because you have a habit of doing dumb things."

I chuckled and leaned in for one last hug. "Take care of Mitchell. I'm pretty fond of him."

"I'm getting pretty attached to him myself."

Reluctantly, I pulled away and got into the cab. Mitchell and Owen had joined Rebecca at the edge of the curb. Mitchell had his arm around her, and she leaned into him as they watched my cab pull away. Owen waved, and the sight of him retreating into the distance made my heart give a funny throb.

The drive wasn't that far, maybe ten minutes or so. I flipped through Joyce's file one last time on the ride, refreshing myself on the details of her life. Before I knew it, the cab stopped at my new apartment and the driver took my luggage upstairs. I followed him, the shoes digging into my heels with each stair we climbed. He set my suitcases down just inside the door, and after I thanked him and tossed the file on a nearby table, we both left. I didn't have time to explore my new digs, but I registered that the place was both furnished and small.

Agusto's office was only a few blocks from the new

apartment, and I spent the walk trying to clear my head, get my defenses in order, and well…get my mind ready for the long road ahead.

Just before I went inside, I touched base with David one last time. *I'm not sure if I should risk talking to you inside. I'm just about to go in. Will advise when I can.*

I didn't wait for an answer before crossing the threshold into enemy territory.

## 12

The building Agusto owned was sprawling, and I wondered how I'd ever learn my way around. Just beyond the glass doors separating safety from the enemy's lair, a receptionist sat at a tall desk against the back wall. Chairs lined the front wall, with plants scattered around. A fountain dominated one of the short walls, and a huge saltwater fish tank helped balance the water feature on the other. It made the room feel rather serene.

"My name is Joyce Nye. I'm here to see Mr. Masterson," I said to the receptionist, standing up as straight as possible to try to exude confidence.

"Of course, Ms. Nye." The woman didn't look familiar. She had straight, brown hair that cropped into a bob, giving her a severe look. But her huge, brown eyes softened her face. I had no way of knowing whether or not this was my ally. All I knew was that the mole was a woman. She could be anyone, and with those kinds of odds, no one could be trusted or confided in.

She picked up the phone and called a mystery person. "Joyce Nye is here." Hanging up without saying goodbye, she pointed me toward one of the chairs in the lobby area. "Someone will be right out to take you to Mr. Masterson."

"Thank you," I said, giving her my friendliest smile. Instead of sitting down, I went to look at the fish tank. In my downtime, watching the colorful fish swim by, I was tempted to reach out to Owen to tell him about the building and my suspicions about the receptionist. But this was the first time we were using our new long-distance communication method in a real mission. If the line wasn't airtight, and she heard me, I'd be dead in the water before I even got to meet Agusto Masterson.

To be fair, I was letting through some mundane thoughts, and I had a fair amount of impressive defenses in place, including the cloak, so the likelihood that she would hear me was slim. Was it worth the risk? A blue tang stopped right in front of my face. "Nope," I told it, reaching my finger up to the glass. It tried to nip at it, making me smile.

But the moment was shattered when a man behind me startled us both. "Joyce Nye?" His voice was too loud for how close he was to me. It echoed.

Taking a calming breath to expel my flash of irritation over being startled, I turned and offered him my hand, but he didn't take it. He looked at it and turned around. "This way."

He was tall, bald, and dressed in a black suit. Even his shirt and tie were black. The only thing that didn't fit into the color scheme was the clear earpiece and the wire that trailed from it, down the back of his neck, and into the back of his suit coat. Security.

Once we were alone in the elevator together, I felt the telltale push against my mind, and I knew he was probing me. I held my breath, hoping my time spent creating Joyce, and then throwing her to the wolves outside the cloak, were enough to throw this dog off my scent.

At least I didn't have to probe him to know he was a reader.

He didn't bother to look back at me at all as we made our way down a long corridor, up a few floors in an elevator, and down another hall that was more nicely decorated than the one downstairs.

It was adorned with plush carpet that looked like it was cleaned and plumped on a daily basis. It also had upgraded light fixtures that cast a soft yellow light on the space, and small fountains coming out of the walls on either side at regular intervals. It created a very Zen, spa-like atmosphere.

Silently, the guard and I walked down the hallway as I wallowed in my disappointment over the guard's abilities. Of course Agusto had surrounded himself with readers. Why wouldn't he, if he was really a high-ranking member of the Potestas? One thing was for sure—this was bound to make my job more difficult.

The guard stopped in front of a set of cherry-wood double doors. He opened them, revealing a grand, circular room. Windows lined the back wall, displaying a glorious view of DC's monuments.

To my amazement, I realized a small river was running through the floor, dividing the room in half. A stone stood in the middle, and the guard stepped easily across it, obviously well practiced. Putting way too much faith in my ability to walk in my torturous shoes, I followed suit, and by some miracle, I made it across without getting my legs wet. I'd always thought the rich had more money than sense, and here was the proof.

Peeking around the guard, I saw Agusto sitting at a huge, cherry desk that faced the windows. His head was down, and he appeared to be writing something.

"Mr. Masterson, the assistant candidate is here."

"Wonderful," he said, rather flatly. He continued writing, and the guard walked away, leaving me alone with a man who didn't seem to want to give me the time of day.

As I watched him take his station near the door, I took a better look at the office and its décor. Huge paintings of men I didn't recognize hung on the walls, and guards stood between them, making me tense. I hadn't originally noticed them because of how still they stood, but it was bad news; I was more outnumbered than I'd originally thought.

Glancing at Agusto to make sure he was still preoccupied, I took care to keep releasing benign thoughts about the gorgeous room and my excitement about potentially working for him.

Carefully, I inspected the guards. Oddly, three of the five who were quietly lining the walls weren't readers. Their unguarded thoughts bombarded me the moment I reached out. Why would Agusto have non-readers so close to him? Why wouldn't he surround himself with only allies, particularly if he was so important to the Potestas' cause? I was so busy scrutinizing the guards, I didn't notice Agusto had turned his attention toward me.

"I hope the guards don't make you uncomfortable. I find their presence..." He trailed off, as if searching for the right word. "Necessary."

I turned back to him and smiled, hoping it would be enough to convince him I wasn't uncomfortable. Instead of smiling back, he held out his hand without standing up, and I stepped forward and took it. His shake was firm and abrupt. A single pump was all he needed before he let me go.

"Nice to meet you, Ms. Nye. I'm Agusto Masterson. Please call me Agusto."

Nodding, I said, "Then you must call me Joyce."

"Fine. Deal struck." Even his causal talk was all business. "You have a very impressive resume, Joyce. Graduated top of your class with an MBA from Stanford. Your first position after graduating was with Apple. Tell me a little bit about what you did for them. I'm not sure how your experience at a technology company would translate here." He sat forward in his chair as I stood uncomfortably in front of him. Although his tone was soft, almost friendly, I definitely felt like I was being interrogated, and I got the impression that was exactly how he wanted it.

"The positions are probably more similar than you would expect. I assisted many of the upper-level managers within the company. I helped them put presentations together, fielded phone calls and errands so they could focus on their teams, tracked deadlines, and helped in any way I could. I was a jack-of-all-trades, so to speak. If something needed to be done, I did it."

"And as a Stanford graduate, you found that work satisfying?"

He was baiting me, but it didn't bother me. I had a response. "For now, yes. I left Apple because I wanted a change of scenery. Nothing more, nothing less. It takes time to climb within a company. I understand that. I'm willing to do the work."

He leaned back in his chair, appraising me. "And what if I hire you and you decide you want another change of scenery?"

"And what if you kick me to the curb after I spend years here, giving it my all? I'm going to be honest with you, Agusto—I'm in this for me, not you. If this job becomes more negative than positive for me at any point, I'll leave with no regrets. But while I'm here, you have me one hundred and ten percent."

He smiled at me, and although I knew I'd taken a risk in saying that, I sensed he would respond to an appeal to his selfish side. After all, he did think his most productive workers were selfishly motivated. As he stood, he held out his hand, and I took it.

"I think you'll be an excellent fit here, Joyce."

I smiled confidently back at him, taking care to hide the gamut of emotions running through my mind. I'd deal with them later.

Abruptly, he released me and went back to his desk, opening a drawer and flipping through some papers. "As my personal assistant, you will do what I ask, when I ask it, without question," he said as he pulled out a form. "With that comes a certain amount of confidentiality. I need to know I can trust you before you will really be useful to me."

"Agreed," I said, not knowing if I should speak or not.

"This is a very detailed confidentiality agreement. I recommend you take it home, read it carefully, and sign it. You will start work once it's been signed. If you would like, have it looked at by a lawyer. It's important for you understand what you're signing away."

*What I'm signing away?* I thought as I glanced over the document in my hands. He had a way of providing you with just enough honesty to make you almost want to trust him. It made me nervous about what he was hiding.

He eyed me and then said, "Trust takes time to build. However, know this. You have my respect until you give me a reason to take it away. Don't abuse that."

"Understood."

Succinctly, he nodded once. "Fine. Come back to me when you're ready to work. And don't take too much time, Joyce. There's a lot to do." With that, he turned his back to me, not even watching as I stood to leave, the confidentiality agreement in hand.

*I guess that's that.* I turned on my heels and walked out as calmly as I could, taking care to make sure my steps were even and unhurried all the way out of his office, downstairs, and out of the building to safety.

I didn't go to my apartment. Instead, I wandered a few blocks over to a café, wanting to get far enough from Agusto's office to be out of range of any spies, but not too far. I ordered a cup of coffee and sat down with the form, reading it over. I tried to skip down to the meat of it, but even then I was bored with the legalese.

*David?* I asked as I scanned the document.

*What, are you done already? Did you blow it?*

*No! Why would you even ask me that? Total confidence in me, huh?* I teased. I knew he was just anxious about how the mission was going, but I couldn't let that one go.

He didn't answer me, and I knew he was waiting for some real information. So I got straight to it. *The job is mine, if I sign this super long and boring confidentiality agreement.*

*We expected that. Make a copy of it before you sign it, just in case you need to reference it later. But go ahead and sign it. After all, Joyce Nye doesn't exist. She can't be legally bound to anything. I've double and triple checked with the attorneys in our system. You'll be fine. He may ask you about it though, so try to read it carefully and understand what it says.*

*Will do.* With that green light, I finished my coffee and studied the rest of the agreement.


Turned out the confidentiality report was everything I expected. Basically I was selling my soul to Agusto and his company, and if I had a problem with that, my only option was to not sign the form. I didn't have the luxury of having a problem with it, so I just signed it, trusting that David was right and the form was the least of my problems.

I made a copy of the form at a local office and returned to the lion's den just after lunch. The receptionist summoned the same guard, who silently ushered me through the various levels of the building and back to Agusto's office.

"You're back quickly. You obviously didn't have a lawyer read it over." His tone was very judgmental, as if I'd already made a misstep.

"Actually, I have a lawyer friend downtown. I went straight from here to her office. She advised me not to sign it. I believe her exact words were: 'No job is worth it.'"

He laughed. "Then why did you sign it?"

"Because I want to work for the great Agusto Masterson. You're trying to save the world after all."

He snorted, and it sounded almost like disgust, but I didn't know him well enough to distinguish his moods yet.

"All right, good. Once you're settled in, take that form

to human resources." I nodded, and he kept talking. "I suppose now is as good a time as any for you to meet one of the most valuable members of my staff. Aside from me, she's the one you'll be working with most."

He turned around and pressed a call button on his phone. "Amanda, come in, won't you? I've selected a new assistant." He didn't wait for her response before turning back around.

*Amanda.* The name hit me like a semi. It couldn't be her. It wouldn't be her. Amanda was a common name.

A door opened that I hadn't noticed in my earlier inspection. It was seamlessly placed between two paintings and a guard. As it was on our side of the river, she didn't have to cross over the rock as she approached us.

My mouth went dry in an instant. *She'll recognize me. I should kill her before she has the chance. Either way, my whole cover is blown. Shit, what do I do?* I didn't chance a glance at the guards; in fact, I didn't take my eyes off her. She was more smartly dressed than the last time we'd seen each other, but the joy seemed to have disappeared from her eyes. They were tired and sunken, her skin seemed to have taken on a sickly tone, and even her hair looked stringy and unhealthy. Something had happened to her, or maybe was happening to her still.

A bony hand reached out to me, and I examined her rail-thin arm. She'd lost weight. "I'm Amanda Pierce. I'm the vice president of Agusto's largest company AMHC."

I looked at her blankly, unable to make my mind process and respond. She was the vice president of his largest company. I remembered Davis saying something about a new VP being recently appointed, but I had never dreamed it would be her. This mission had just become a minefield for me, and I suddenly wished someone else had been chosen.

"Well, Agusto, seems like you picked an intelligent one," Amanda said. Clearly, whatever disappointments or setbacks she'd faced hadn't affected her sarcasm and contempt for others.

Agusto smiled at us, seemingly enjoying the verbal thrashing. "Amanda takes her job very seriously. She's learned what's at stake when you work for me. Soon, you will too."

*Was that a threat?* My mind was awhirl, and I was having trouble keeping up. I dreaded the moment I'd have to speak in front of her. Surely, she would recognize my voice. By some miracle, the Unseen's disguise seemed to be good enough to fool a woman I'd lived with for eighteen years. But my voice would undoubtedly give the whole thing away.

"Amanda will show you around today, and she'll help you get your work phone set up so I can reach you easily. I'll let you know when you are needed. Enjoy." With that, he turned back around, leaving Amanda and me staring at his back, except she didn't look for long. She turned and walked briskly away, leaving me to scurry to catch up to her.

Her office was significantly smaller than Agusto's. Long and narrow, it only had a few windows on the back wall, and it was much more sparsely decorated. The river disappeared beneath the wall between the rooms.

"What happened to the river?" I asked, and then slammed my mouth shut, angry with myself for letting curiosity overcome my common sense. I hadn't even tried to mask my voice or add an accent.

*Well, that's done it. Pack your bags, you're going home...if you're lucky and she doesn't have it out with you right here, right now.*

Curiosity clouded her expression, as if something nagged at the back of her mind. She ignored it, for the moment. "Agusto doesn't come into my office, so the river doesn't need to be in here." Her tone was short, as if the answer was so obvious she couldn't believe I'd wasted her time with the question.

Taking a breath, I hoped I could gather some patience

if I was to spend so much time with her in the coming weeks. I wasn't mentally prepared to work so closely with someone I'd spent my life trying to escape, so it took some work to get my mind right.

Her small desk near the windows faced out into the room, and the office was decorated with a few plants, a floor lamp in one corner, bookshelves lining one wall, and a plush chair. That was it. It was nice, but after seeing the grandeur that was Agusto's office, it fell a little short for me. I almost felt bad for her, having that dichotomy rubbed in her face every time she went in there. It was like a constant message that she wasn't as good as Agusto, and therefore wasn't as deserving.

"You will not have an office. You won't need it. You will be much too busy and mobile for that. Everything you need will be kept in here, files and things of that nature. If you need access to a computer, there's a lab downstairs you can use. Come with me, and I'll show you."

We walked out and down the hall to the elevator. While we were there, she handed me a card. "That's your keycard, so you can get back up to the executive level."

For the first time, I noticed there was a slot below the numbers on the elevator's keypad. I had hadn't noticed it on the way up, both times. *Reasons I probably should've been paying attention instead of feeling out the guard's mind.*

"I don't have time to hold your hand and give you a tour of the entire building," she said as the elevator came to a stop, "but I'm going to show you where you can find the things you'll need most." She led the way out, keeping such an intense pace, I had trouble keeping up with her. It was even worse than walking with Tracy through the airport on our first mission together. At least I'd been comfortable with Tracy.

We didn't go in any of the rooms, she simply gestured to them as we walked by. "There's the computer lab. This is the cafeteria, although there are some good places to eat outside this building too, if you can afford it." She smiled sidelong at me, as if looking down her nose.

I let the comment roll off me, trying to concentrate on absorbing everything she was saying, but the pace of the tour was too frantic. I knew I'd have to ask for directions when she wasn't around.

We walked to the end of the long hall and entered a huge, cold room, with machines stacked all the way to the ceiling for what seemed like hundreds of yards. "This is our IT department. They will issue you your work phone and all your security clearances. I'm going to leave you here for a few moments. Think you can manage?" I answered her condescending tone with a sweet smile. She responded by rolling her eyes and walking away in a huff.

I exhaled when she was gone, releasing some of the tension I'd been feeling since her sudden appearance in Agusto's office.

*Get a hold of yourself. You'll give yourself away if you're not careful. Take a breath. She hasn't recognized you yet. Just step carefully and you should be fine...at least for long enough to get what you need and get out.*

Standing up a little straighter, I walked the short distance to the man sitting at the desk in the front corner of the room. Apparently, he was very involved in whatever task he was doing, because he didn't look away from his computer as I approached.

I cleared my throat, but that didn't work either, so I resorted to speaking to him. "Um, I'm supposed to get my phone and security clearance from you?"

"Name?" His eyes were still glued to the computer.

"Joyce Nye."

"Card, please." It was a statement, not a request.

I handed over the keycard Amanda had given me, and he inserted it into a slot in his computer. "You'll have limited access to most areas of the company, including servers and network access. Put your card in the slot next to the computer you'd like to use, and you're set." He removed the card and handed it back to me, finally making impatient eye contact.

I grabbed the card from him, not wanting to occupy more of his time than was necessary. He went back to his computer, leaving me rather awkwardly standing there.

"Um...the phone."

Reluctantly, he looked at me and audibly sighed. It pushed me over the edge. "Look, I know everyone in this company has a ridiculously high work ethic, and whatever you're doing is a million times more important than dealing with me, but for right now, *I'm your job*. Take care of me, and I'll be out of your hair a lot faster than if you keep on giving me attitude."

He rolled his eyes so hard I almost asked him what his brain looked like, but then he opened a drawer beneath him. Pulling out a very expensive smartphone, he started toggling from screen to screen. "I'll let you set up your own password," he finally said. "Your company email is on here, as well as Internet access. I'm setting up your clearance level now, and you should be good to go. Agusto's number is already programmed into it. His is the only saved number, so it's not hard to find."

As soon as he held the phone out to me, I took it from him. "Thank you." I hoped I'd find at least one friendly person within Agusto's company. But I wasn't there to make friends. I was there to do a job. Making friends would probably just make that job harder.

*I should just adapt a cold personality, like everyone else here*, I thought. *It'd be safer.*

Amanda was walking toward the IT room at a breakneck speed just as I was leaving. "Good. You're done. Let's grab a coffee."

Again, I was thrown off. She wanted to do something social? She'd acted so annoyed with me, so why would she want to get coffee? Or maybe she didn't. Maybe Agusto had asked her to do it. I sighed internally, deciding that maybe she just took pleasure in keeping the people around her off balance.

We walked to a little cafe just around the corner from the office. "We have twenty minutes before I have to be at a meeting, and you should start learning your way around."

*She's telling me to hurry up and drink my coffee,* I thought.

We sat down at a small table near the window. She ordered black coffee. Didn't even put any sugar in it. Very utilitarian, get the job done with as little frills as possible. I, on the other hand, liked frills, especially when it came to coffee, so I ordered the most sugary drink on the menu, completed with whipped cream and caramel sauce on top. She frowned as I sipped my drink, but I didn't care. It was delicious.

"Tell me about yourself. Where do you come from? What's your background?"

"I grew up in Colorado. I graduated from Stanford a few years ago, worked for Apple for a while, and now I'm here. Not a terribly interesting story."

"So, you're ambitious. What made you leave Apple?"

"I was ready for a change of scenery. Plus, California is so expensive." I shrugged as I sipped my drink again.

She frowned as she watched me. "Not the brightest choice, I would say."

"Intelligence has nothing to do with it. Not the safest choice? Maybe. Not the best choice for my career? Debatable. But it wasn't stupid."

Her mouth hung open for a few beats, then she closed it and smiled. "I think I'm going to like you."

Relaxing a little, I ate my lunch in silence for a bit. Then she asked me another question.

"You're really from Colorado, huh? I had you pegged as a Florida girl. You sound just like someone I knew who grew up there."

My heart stopped for a moment, and I struggled not to show my distress outwardly. *Keep drinking your coffee, swallow, and smile at her. Don't give her a reason to suspect you, now that you've finally started to build a relationship.*

I just nodded as I sipped my drink, and after a

moment, she glanced at her watch. "We'd better go. You're on your own for the rest of the day. I'll check in with you a little later. Where's your phone?" I pulled it out of my pocket and handed it to her, grateful this suit had pockets at all, let alone ones big enough for a smartphone.

She punched in her information with so much vehemence, I felt sorry for the phone. Tossing it back onto the table, she said, "There, now you have my number. Text me if you need anything." She got up and gathered her things, then turned to look back at me. "Are you coming?"

For a second, I'd thought she would give me a moment alone. But no, she stood there waiting for me, so I stood and followed her back across enemy lines.

By the time we got back, there wasn't much time left in the day, but I decided to spend it exploring the building, trying to learn where things were. The first floor was where the computer lab and cafeteria were located. The second floor mostly consisted of the offices of people who worked under the AMHC umbrella. I tried to introduce myself to a few of them, but they were all pretty cold. The third floor was the executive area. I didn't know who else was up there, so I decided not to poke around. I didn't feel the need to get fired on my first day.

I carefully probed the people I passed to get a feel of what I was up against. It turned out to be a mixed bag of readers and non-readers, split almost evenly by my count. If Agusto's company really was a Potestas' hotbed, why weren't they all readers?

By five o'clock, I was feeling good about the building itself, but I hadn't heard a peep from Agusto. Amanda finally texted me.

*How's it going?*

*Good! I think I've learned my way around.*

*Good. What did you get done today?*

...*I learned my way around.* What else had she expected me to do? It wasn't like anyone had assigned me any tasks.

*That's it?* I could feel her eyes rolling through the phone.

*That's it. But I did it well.*

*Well, good. See you in the morning.* It was too hard to detect her tone via text. I could only hope I was still on her good side.

*Is it weird that Agusto hasn't been in touch?*

*No. He needs to trust you.*

*How can he trust me if I never see him?*

*Don't be impatient. Pretty soon he'll be texting you more than you want. I'm done talking to you now.*

I couldn't help but chuckle at her response. I could practically hear the snark in her voice as I read the message.

Relieved to be, well, relieved, I walked out of the building and headed back to my apartment. I kept my phone on, just in case either of them needed anything that night. I hoped I hadn't squandered the only day I'd have alone by learning the layout of the building and scoping out the enemy. I could've gone deeper and potentially learned more, but I was trying to be discreet. And the guy I really needed to get to know wasn't quite ready to let me into his circle.

As I climbed the stairs to my apartment, exhaustion flooded me. I still needed to touch base with David and the others, but I was so tired. I'd been up long before sunrise, after getting very little sleep for the past two nights, and the stress of the day was wearing on me.

Just as I put the key into the door, my phone buzzed.

*Bring me a Reuben.* It was from Agusto. It didn't say where he was, but I knew better than to question him. He was probably still at the office. If he wasn't there, then I'd start asking. There was a risk I'd waste time, but they needed to know I was willing to figure stuff out on my own.

*Be there in 15 or less*, I texted back. I'd really be S.O.L. if he wasn't in his office, but it was best to dive in with both feet, right?

Taking the key out of the door, I turned and ran back down the stairs, searching for the closest deli on my phone as I went. I ran to the shop, ordered a Reuben, some chips, and a drink to be safe, and hustled back to the office. I arrived outside the cherry double doors with two minutes to spare, but I was pretty sure my feet were bloodied from the experience.

Because I was supposed to be there, I didn't knock before entering. I walked into the room with confidence, maneuvered over the river without dropping his meal into the water, and stopped at his desk. Luckily for me, he was sitting there with his back to me, but I didn't dare breathe a sigh of relief for having guessed correctly.

"Your dinner."

"Set it over there." He nodded toward the end of his desk. I found a clear spot and set it down. Lining the back of his desk, a myriad of books was jammed between two silver bookends that looked like an arrow piercing them. He had Machiavelli's *The Prince*, an alarming number of books on politics that I hoped he would never want to discuss with me, and a few fiction titles I didn't recognize. I'd never been much of a reader, well, of literature anyway. Maddie would've known what they were.

"Anything else?" I asked, wondering if I should just leave or await further instructions.

"If there is anything else, I will tell you."

Ignoring his sharp tone and lack of eye contact, I nodded to him. "Have a good night."

He didn't respond as I made my way back out of his office.

I was standing in front of my apartment, my key once again poised outside the lock, when my phone chimed.

*Black coffee. Now.*

"Couldn't you have asked me for that earlier?" I glanced at my watch. It was almost six. David probably wouldn't be too worried about me yet, but I chanced a quick message to him anyway.

*Being tested. Will touch base when I can.*

There was a coffee shop right across the street from the building, so I limped over and returned to Agusto's office with the coffee in record time.

I set the coffee next to him on his desk, and then left without comment.

When I arrived back in front of my apartment for the third time that night, I hesitated in front of the door, waiting for my phone to chirp. By some miracle, it didn't, so I ventured inside.

Finally, I peeled the shoes off my feet and surveyed the room. It was small, nothing more than a studio, but it was trendy, clean, and safe. The kitchen had zero counter space, a less-than-full-sized refrigerator, a stovetop, and a microwave. There was no dishwasher. I shrugged. I had the company card, paid for by the Unseen. I could afford to eat out some, and I knew from experience that I could survive on cereal. I'd be fine. My luggage was stacked neatly near the door, the bathroom was across from the kitchen, and the living room/bedroom completed the tour.

The bed was dressed in flowing, white linens, and right now, it looked glorious. A television sat across from it, stacked on top of a short, four-drawer dresser.

After double and triple checking the locks, I made my way to the bed. *Owen?*

*Oh my God. We've been waiting for hours to hear back from you.*

*I was surrounded. I didn't want to risk it. How's it going?*

*Slow. We didn't get anything done today because none of us could focus.*

*Understandable,* I said, picturing myself in Owen's place. No way would I have been useful. I would have been a nervous wreck.

*I'm home, guys,* I said, reaching out to David and Rebecca, pulling them into the conversation.

*Owen's just told me,* David said. *I'm glad. What's the good word?*

*Amanda is his VP.* I dropped the bomb casually.

Silence was his only answer, and I knew he was thinking about what it meant for the mission.

*Did she recognize you?* Owen asked.

*No. But my voice is naggingly familiar to her. It could be a problem.*

*How closely do you have to work with her?* David asked

*Close. I spent more time with her than with Agusto today. And I think that'll be the norm. Honestly, I think she likes Joyce.*

*Good. Keep it that way,* David said.

*Rebecca, you there?* I asked.

*Just processing,* she said.

*He also has an odd mix of readers and non-readers around him. About half of the guards I met today were non-readers. Why wouldn't he want to be surrounded by his allies? Think about Shields. Potestas were crawling all over that park when we saw him. Plus, as far as he knows, he just hired a non-reader as his assistant. Why would he hire non-readers at all, let alone position them close to him?*

David answered me. *That is interesting. Maybe he doesn't trust those around him?*

*Does that include Amanda?* I thought about her elevated position and her haggard appearance. Was she doing her penance with Agusto? What did that mean for who he was within the organization? Was he some kind of warden?

*I don't know,* David said. *For our part, we don't have anything new. We were…less than productive today.*

*So I heard,* I answered, chuckling to myself. *I'm fine, guys. Don't worry. Admittedly, I could hardly speak when Amanda came through that door. I mean, of all people… It went fine after that, though. I'll have to be on my toes, but this wasn't a pleasure cruise from the get-go, was it?*

*No, otherwise I'd be there with you,* Owen said.

A glance at my watch told me it was almost seven. *I don't suppose you could meet me for dinner?*

David answered for Owen. *No. It's too risky. You have to*

*maintain your cover.*

*Fine. But can you send some flats my way? These shoes are a freaking joke if I'm going to be running across town six times a day to get that lazy man food.*

*Flats?* David asked.

*I'll take care of it,* Rebecca interjected.

*I'm going to let you say good night to Owen. We'll talk in the morning,* David said.

Rebecca signed off too, leaving Owen and me alone.

*This connection thing is kind of nice,* I thought.

*Yeah, someone pretty smart must've come up with it.*

*I bet you'd like to date her.*

*Nah. Two women are quite enough for me.* He couldn't stifle his laugh, not even in his head. It was frustrating not to be nearby so I could smack him…and then do other things.

*What now?* he asked.

*I keep working for Agusto until I find something. And I get something to eat.*

We said our goodbyes, and I finally got some food. I crawled into bed around nine, which was early for me, but I was exhausted.

Unfortunately for me, my sleep was interrupted around midnight. A text alert startled me awake. Confusion clouded my mind as I tried to decide if I'd dreamed the sound or not. Blindly, I reached for my phone, knocking it off the nightstand next to me.

*Black coffee. Now.*

I read it again. Was it some kind of network glitch? It was exactly the same message from earlier that day. But could I really risk ignoring it if it wasn't a glitch? Sighing, I got up, pulled on some sweats and a T-shirt—at midnight, he wasn't getting a suit and high heels—fumbled with my nose, contacts, and makeup, and headed a block over to the twenty-four-hour cafe. Google was saving my skin. By the time I doubled back to the office and made my way through the dark building, a record fourteen minutes had passed. But it was hard to care at almost 12:30 at night.

Much to my chagrin, his office door was locked. Either it was a glitch, or he was really testing me. If it was the latter, the 12 AM text was quite enough, thank you.

Amanda's door was open, so I went in that way and used the secret door to Agusto's office.

Guards still lined the walls of his office, so I knew right away he was there.

No surprise, Agusto was at his desk. Neither of us acknowledged the other. He didn't look up from his computer, and I simply put the cup in its usual spot and walked away.

Before I got to the door, he stopped me. "Joyce."

I stopped dead, but I didn't give him the satisfaction of turning around. "A little faster next time, hmm? You don't want to find out what happens to those who disappoint me."

The threat made me turn to look at him. "Why don't you just tell me so I don't have to learn the hard way?"

"If you really want to know, why don't you speak to Amanda?" A sick grin spread across his face as he turned back to his computer, absently grabbing his fresh coffee and taking a sip.

It was hard to control my breathing and posture on my way out of the room. Once I was safely inside Amanda's office, I leaned against the door, taking a moment to compose myself.

*I can do this*, I assured myself as I walked home and let myself into the apartment. Midnight coffee calls were nothing. Just try to stay on his good side. What had he meant about Amanda though? Something told me her haggard appearance wasn't unrelated. What exactly had he done to her after she'd "disappointed" him? Sighing, I climbed back into bed. I wasn't going to solve the mystery then, and the more I stewed about it, the less sleep I'd get. But every time I closed my eyes, I saw her sunken, red-rimmed eyes.

Of course, I could guess why she'd gotten on his bad

side. She'd let me escape, and Dylan's death would have fallen on her shoulders. I could never ask her what Agusto had done to her. I'd just have to assume the worst and do my best to stay on Agusto's good side.

Sighing, I rolled over and looked at the clock. 3:26 blared at me. I shook my head, rolled back over, and put my back to the clock. Why should I care about Amanda anyway? Surely, everything she'd done to me outweighed whatever had happened to her. She'd probably deserved it, right?

The eye-for-an-eye mentality did little to comfort me, so I rustled around for my iPod, plugged in my headphones, and let Gaspard carry me through the long night.

# 13

The next week passed in a blur. Agusto was preparing for a big press conference, though only he seemed to know what he was going to say. He only spoke to me when he wanted something. So he didn't tell me any trade secrets, and I was on my own to find out anything I could about Zero—which was nothing.

Frustratingly, he kept at least two guards with him at all times. They even went into the bathroom with him. Picturing them standing at the urinal stalls on either side of Agusto just made me uncomfortable. It was evidence that he didn't feel safe, even on the pot.

At first, I tried my best to keep Amanda at arm's length, thinking the less interactions we had, the less likely she would be to recognize me. But, as time went on, I discovered how impossible it was to keep my distance from her. We worked too closely together. She was more like Agusto's main assistant than the VP of AMHC.

Later in the week, I decided to ask her about it. "You sure spend an awful lot of time waiting on Agusto considering you're VP of one of his biggest companies. Don't you need to, you know, help run AMHC?"

"Thankfully, I have more competent people than you

working for me. They do their jobs without hand holding."

All I could do was smile and shake my head. Although she seemed to be slowly warming to me, she never lost her I'm-better-than-you snark.

On Friday, after we'd spent all week hustling for Monday's press conference, Amanda was particularly short. I knew she needed to pick up some documents from Kinkos for Monday, so I offered to do it for her, hoping to solidify our relationship. If I couldn't keep her at bay, maybe I could learn something from her. After all, Agusto wasn't telling me anything.

She looked at me like I had six heads, like the thought to ask *me* for help had never occurred to her.

Her face hardened, and I thought she might refuse. "You think I need *your* help?"

"Nope, I just wanted something to do."

"Well, if it would help fill your time, then by all means. Go."

Smiling to myself as I walked out, I knew I'd made some headway. I spent the rest of the day helping her out, and that weekend she texted me instructions to pick up a few last-minute things on my way in Monday morning. Positioning myself as an asset to her would hopefully prove helpful.

All week, the Unseen hadn't gotten anywhere with their research, and since I hadn't learned anything either, we were getting a little frustrated. Rebecca was the only one who didn't seem bothered by our lack of progress. She reminded everyone that I had to learn Agusto's routines, gain his trust, and get to know him before I would be afforded the opportunity to see anything unusual.

But after a lonely weekend, I was ready to wrap up my mission. I'd taken my laundry to a cleaner, walked around some of the monuments, and spent way too much time whining to Owen about being alone.

I did find a piano shop on Sunday night. The owner said I could play for as long as I wanted, and he even stopped by the piano to listen. The music helped calm my nerves, so I went into the office on Monday morning feeling focused.

The press was buzzing with speculation on what he would announce, and I was just as anxious as they were. Both he and Amanda had been tight-lipped about the announcement, leaving me totally in the dark.

Finally, he approached the podium to make his speech. "Thank you for coming, everyone. My fellow Americans, we have something to celebrate." The sparkle in his eye made me nervous, but Amanda, who stood close to me, showed no emotion at all.

"After analyzing the sample of Zero obtained at the USCF Medical Center, we were able to apprehend a suspect."

Murmuring spread through the audience, but he held up a hand to cut it short. "There is evidence of his involvement in the plot, so there is reason hope he may have information on the next attack.

"Now, this does not mean the threat is over. He is one man in what I believe to be a large organization. But, I've found a chink in their armor. It's hope.

"My plan is to learn what we use to stop the next attack, which will get us that much closer to ending this thing altogether.

"I'm sorry, but I will not be taking questions today. You will be advised when we know more. Thank you for your time."

*Holy shit,* I thought as Agusto walked past me, smiling like a snake his whole way out of the room. The press was a flurry of activity as they frantically composed their stories.

"He has a suspect? How was that not important information for me to know?" I whispered to Amanda.

"What exactly would you have done with it? How would it have changed your day-to-day responsibilities?"

"I suppose it wouldn't, but this is huge."

"Not really," she said, and the flatness of her tone made me question the news.

"Not really?"

"Let's just say he's got his sights aimed a little higher than Zero right now. This publicity will help him get there."

That statement made me stop for a moment. "What does that mean?"

"It means we need to finish up here, so we can move on to the next task."

The comment bothered me, but I didn't say that to Amanda. She seemed to be one hundred percent behind Agusto. Whether she actually respected him was another thing altogether. The way she never made eye contact with him told me she feared him. But why? And what did it have to do with his next task?

That night, I mentioned it to David and the others as I paced restlessly around my small apartment.

*I'm starting to suspect he may be positioning himself for presidential candidacy*, David said.

*What? No.* David's words settled in the pit of my stomach like bad Chinese food.

*What evidence do we have to support that assumption?* Owen asked, looking for reasons to deny it with me.

*The fact that he's so focused on becoming a prominent public figure. He obviously wants to be seen as a savior—the man who's rescued the world from Zero. Then there's the fundraising he's been doing. And the fact that Mackenzie was told the Potestas were aiming for a position of power. If they got one of their top officials into the presidential seat...* His thought trailed off.

A top member of the Potestas in the presidential seat. With that kind of power in the hands of a terrorist, it could easily mean the end of the country as we knew it. Who knew what they'd do with the power.

Easing myself onto my bed, I tried to comprehend what it might mean, but I couldn't. All I could see was horror.

*How do we stop it?* I asked, wishing they were all with me. I suddenly felt so alone in my little apartment.

*Find out what we can, as fast as we can. We need proof. But not proof of his candidacy. Proof that he's bad news*, Owen offered.

*Is it time to just go in?* I asked, nervous about the prospect. He was never unguarded, and there was no way his guards would just let me hack into his head. They would have to be taken care of first.

Rebecca piped up. *This is no time to be hasty. The election isn't for over a year. Let's wait until we can be better armed.*

I wasn't sure how I felt about that. Going in right away meant the mission would be over faster, and I could go home sooner. But it would also be riskier. Taking an unnecessary risk might mean I wouldn't get to go home at all.

*Don't you think I'll have to go in eventually anyway?* I asked.

*Yes. But waiting might benefit us.*

I didn't know what to think. *It's going to be messy, no matter how long we wait*, I told them.

A long pause followed. David was the one who ultimately broke the silence. *I think we should wait. Rebecca is right. It's only been a week. We have time to build a case against him before the election.*

*If we wait too long, I could make a mistake and blow this opportunity for good. The longer I'm here, the more familiar Amanda and I will get, and the more likely that is to happen.*

*Quit it*, Owen interjected. *You're better than that and you know it, so stop the pity party. Do your job—get in, get out, and get it done.*

I wasn't used to hearing him talk like that, but it was exactly what I needed at the moment. *You channeling Tracy?*

*Maybe.*

We argued about it for a while longer, but the decision had been made. We would wait.

*And what about the suspect?* I asked.

*There is no evidence that anyone has been apprehended or is in custody. Much like there is no evidence that he had any Zero to analyze in the first place,* Owen said. *But he has enough people in his pocket to get away with the lie.*

*What would he get out of lying about that?* I asked.

Rebecca answered quickly. *Plenty. He gets the trust of the nation, without the need to actually follow through. Besides, if we're correct in our assumption that he's a high-ranking official for the Potestas, he doesn't really need to have a suspect in hand. He'll still be able to "stop" the next attack.* I could hear the air quotes around the word *stop* in her internal dialogue.

*This is less than ideal,* I thought to them all. And that was putting it kindly.

*Agreed, but it doesn't change anything. We need evidence and information. Nothing more, nothing less,* David said.

After that rather bleak revelation, there wasn't much left to say, and everyone started dropping off from the conversation. Eventually, Owen and I were the only ones left.

*Christmas is only a week away.* It came out sadder than I'd intended. It was much harder to guard your thoughts than it was your words.

*That's not a reason to rush into anything, especially if it gets you hurt…or worse,* Owen said. It was a more practical attitude than I'd expected from him, but again, it was what I needed to hear.

*It's our first Christmas together.*

*We will celebrate when this is over. I promise.*

By the time we said goodbye, I was resigned to my fate. Seemed like it would be a long haul, but I was in it to win it. Agusto wouldn't be president if I had anything to say about it. I would make it a Christmas to remember.

# 14

The following day, Amanda and I were having lunch at the same cafe where we'd first had coffee together. We got a lot of our meals there. They met all of Amanda's requirements: They were fast, nutritious, and reliable.

She smiled at me.

"What?" I asked, a little uncomfortable. Her smiles almost never meant anything good.

"You know, when I first met you, you grated on me. Your voice is so similar to that girl I knew. Even some of the phrases you use. But I'm glad I was forced to get to know you. Thankfully, you're nothing like her, save for your voice."

It took some work to accept her backhanded compliment, and even more work not to show a negative reaction. "I'm glad I don't annoy you...too much."

"I have something for you." She pulled out a sealed brown envelope. "I need you to deliver this to Agusto. It contains highly sensitive information meant only for him. Please see that he gets it immediately." We hadn't finished eating, but she started to gather her things. "I'm off to check on some of the major hospitals out west. I'll be back in a few days."

"Wait, what? Why is this the first I'm hearing about this?" I asked, scrambling to keep up with her.

"I figured it was need-to-know information. This landed in my lap, and I have to leave to catch my flight, so suddenly you needed to know." She was so matter-of-fact about it; I didn't know how to respond.

"If you need anything, text me," she added. "If I think it's important enough, I'll respond."

"Well, have a safe trip." She nodded and left me alone in the cafe. The envelope sat on the table in front of me. I looked it over, knowing I should get up and deliver it, but wanting desperately to open it.

What if it was about Zero? If it held the proof we needed to take Agusto down, I wouldn't even have to sneak into his mind. I'd have solid evidence with very little risk.

I chanced a glance around as I picked up the envelope. None of Agusto's employees were there. I was alone.

*David?* I asked as I thumbed the seal on the envelope.

*What? Why are you contacting me in the middle of the day?*

*Amanda has just left me with an envelope to be delivered to Agusto. She said it contains highly sensitive information. Think I should open it?*

Before he could answer me, I sent him another thought. *What if it has the proof we need to shut him down?*

*Okay, let's be logical about this. Why would she tell you there was sensitive information in it? Has she ever told you anything about what you're ferrying around for them?*

I hesitated. *No.* They never gave me an explanation or reason for anything. They barely even acknowledged me when I dropped something off for them.

*Do you think she was trying to tempt you to open it?*

*I don't know,* I said. I felt like a child being scolded.

*Because this is so out of character, I think you should deliver the note undamaged. It feels like a trust exercise to me. If you do it right in their eyes, you may gain more in the long run.*

*But what if it's something huge? The name of the person they're supposedly holding? Evidence about Zero? Or where they plan to attack next?*

*And what if it's not? What if it's just his sandwich order, and all he wants is to see if you opened it?*

Feeling defeated, I gathered my things and left the cafe, the envelope tucked under my arm. *One of these days, you're going to have to let me take a risk, even if it's wrong.*

*Not today.* I tried not to visibly roll my eyes as I went back into Agusto's building and took the elevator to the third floor.

As I stood outside his office, I considered my options. I was a grown woman. David couldn't tell me what to do all the time. Of course, the times I'd gone rogue hadn't exactly served me well—or anyone else, for that matter. But what if this was different? What if breaking the rules was the only way to play the game?

I hesitated outside his office for just another moment, trying to gather my resolve when one of the guards opened the doors, nearly hitting me in the face.

"It's rude to lurk in doorways," he said as he held the doors open for me.

"How did you even know I was out here?" I knew the answer, of course—they must've heard my outgoing thoughts. I'd gotten so good at letting them flow in the background, I often forgot I was doing it at. Had I reined them in, I could've stood there for as long as I wanted.

*Should've, could've, would've,* I thought as I walked across the office. I considered dropping the envelope in the river and destroying the sensitive information it might contain. But I was so close to completing the task, I might as well carry it through to the end. Anyway, why chance "disappointing" him, if it really was just a sandwich order.

I slapped it on his desk a little too hard. If I'd still had long hair, it would've been blown away from my face from the force of the movement. I didn't acknowledge the overly aggressive move, I only said, "Amanda had to leave to catch her flight, so she asked me to deliver this."

He sat back in his chair and peered up at me, amusement on his face. I kept my face cool as I turned to walk out, feeling like I'd made a mistake. But this was a situation in which there were no obvious right answers. As I made my way across the room, I could feel him looking at me. I kept walking.

He called out to me right as I stepped onto the stepping stone in the river.

"One more thing."

*Great.* Now *how am I supposed to turn around?* I had to go across and come back, risking two falls in the river. By some miracle, I made it, but I stopped at the river's edge, not wanting to get any closer to him.

"Your life is about to get much busier."

"How's that?" I asked, not sure I wanted to hear what he was about to say.

"In the spirit of Christmas, I'm going to be announcing my candidacy for the upcoming presidential election when Amanda returns. She'll be my campaign manager, and you will help us win."

I worked hard to school my emotions, but I knew he would expect some response from me. Should I congratulate him? Probably not. He wouldn't want reassurance from lesser employees. How was I supposed to respond? *Very good, sir.* That sounded too much like a butler. *No! You'll destroy this country.* I nearly laughed out loud at that one. But this was no laughing matter, and besides, he was still staring at me.

"Just let me know what's expected of me."

"Oh, I will. I will shape this country into the greatest empire that ever existed. But to do that, we'll have to break some things down first. You need to clean out the parasites, get yourself strong before you can start building back up, don't you agree?" That sinister smile was back, and it turned my stomach.

"I don't know that my opinion much matters."

"You are so right."

"Just…" I hesitated, wondering if I should continue. It almost certainly wasn't wise, but I'd already started.

"Just?"

"Just don't forget what happened to the Romans."

Standing from his chair, he narrowed his gaze at me as he crossed the room. "Don't forget what happened to the Romans?" he asked slowly, drawing the question out as he drew closer to me.

He got so close that his belly was nearly touching me as I stood at the edge of the river, unable to back away. I stifled a swallow, not wanting to show any weakness. "You know that whole, the higher they build it, the farther they fall mentality? I would hate to see you fall."

"Would you?" He backed off a step. "Well, isn't that nice to hear?" The condescension in his voice was evident. He turned on his heels and walked back to his desk. "If ever I need or want your opinion on my life choices, I'll let you know."

I turned and misjudged the distance to the stepping stone, planting my foot firmly in the river. It was ice-cold and about ankle deep, flowing gently against my foot. Taking a breath to steady myself, I planted my other foot on the stone and continued on, knowing he'd heard me splash in the river. He probably felt very satisfied with himself.

I didn't care. I had bigger fish to fry, namely him. It was only one o'clock, but I walked out of his office and left the building. If he needed me, he'd text. I had to talk to David and the others. And get a dry pair of shoes.

# 15

*You were right*, I said to anyone who was listening. They all answered me at almost the same time.

*What's up?*

*He's announcing his candidacy early next week, I guess. After Amanda gets back from her trip out west, but before Christmas. We're running out of time.*

David was the first to try to calm me. *We don't have any less time than we did before. Just because we have confirmation of our suspicions, doesn't mean we need to rush into anything.*

*He's getting bolder about his threats to me.*

*What?* Owen said with obvious heat in his voice.

*It makes me feel the urgency a little more than you guys do.*

*Just try to stay calm. I don't see him making any moves on you as long as you can manage to stay on his good side. What did you do to make him threaten you today?* David asked.

*I reminded him about what happened to Rome.*

*You brought failure to the forefront of his mind?* Rebecca said, amusement in her voice.

*I suppose so, yes.*

*Perhaps a less inflammatory approach might be best in the future?* David asked.

*Whatever, you guys aren't here. You're not living it every day like I am.*

*Okay, let's think about this realistically,* Owen said. *He might not even make it past the primaries. He doesn't have any experience at all in politics. What's the likelihood that the American people will get behind him? Just because he's a smart businessman, doesn't mean he's equipped to run the country.*

I stomped up the stairs to my apartment and let myself inside, slamming the door behind me. *But if he eliminates Zero just in time for the election, think how people will rally behind him. Do you know what he said to me today? That he needed to clean out the parasites before he could build the country into an empire.*

No one responded right away.

*It doesn't change anything, Mackenzie.* David said. *We already knew he was bad news. It stands to reason that he'd have some pretty terrible things planned for his term as president. Just because he implied it out loud doesn't change anything.*

*No, but it wasn't easy to hear.*

*Fair enough,* he said.

I could tell the conversation was over, and they were leaving me alone again. Owen was the only one who stayed behind.

*Just try to hang in there,* Owen said.

*And how's that working out for you?*

*Some days are better than others,* he admitted. *They're right, you know? We have time. Just because he's going to declare he's running, doesn't mean he's going to become president any time soon. It doesn't give him any more power right now.*

*I know. But I can see what he's planning...and it's going to work.*

*We'll stop him before it gets that far. Have a little faith,* he said. I knew he couldn't see me, but I nodded anyway. He was right. I need to stop panicking, take a deep breath, and have a little faith.

Over the next few days, while I waited for Amanda to come back, I found myself repeating that phrase a lot.

"My fellow Americans, I stand before you today to make a very special announcement, in the spirit of the season." The tastefully decorated room was packed, and he'd booked a larger space than normal for the occasion. Every radio, TV station, and Internet news provider was there, anxiously awaiting the great Agusto Masterson's announcement. It was nauseating.

"You've trusted me to eliminate the threat of Zero. And I've shown you that I will not rest until my promise is fulfilled. Now, I'd like you to trust me with something else."

I held my breath as I waited for him to say the words.

"Today, I'm announcing my presidential bid as an independent candidate."

*Independent?* I'd expected him to align himself with a party. I wasn't sure if a third-party candidate had ever won before. It was a huge risk, and it gave me some hope that he might lose after all.

From where I stood at the back of the room, I could easily see the monitors showing the live feed; they displayed with his fancy new website running along the bottom of the screen.

"Right now, I'd like to briefly outline some of my policies for you. If you want more detailed information, please visit the website you see on your screen.

"First and foremost, it would be my priority as president to eliminate terrorist threats to not only our country, but around the world."

*What happened to you taking care of that before you were elected?* I thought, frowning.

"What's wrong with you? You look like you ate a lemon," Amanda whispered.

I just shook my head, trying to rid my face of the expression, and kept listening.

"I would constantly work to ensure that even after the eradication of Zero, no other threats pop up to threaten our great nation. I will keep you safe."

Cheers erupted from the crowd, making my nausea return and intensify.

"Second, I will adopt a logical approach to policies across the board. Science has indicated that there is life before birth, so I will not support abortion of any kind. I will close the borders to our neighbors and implement stricter immigration policies to keep our lands safe. With that, I intend to divert money spent on illegal immigrants to things like free healthcare and education. We must focus on taking care of our own.

"I will stimulate our economy by cutting taxes for the lower and middle class, adding jobs where I can. As a businessman, I can also promise to balance our budget before the end of my term. I can't promise to get this country out of debt, but I can stop digging us deeper into it.

"Now, I know I can't accomplish all of this right away, let alone without help. But I like to set lofty goals. They make victory that much sweeter."

The speech was so brutally honest that I feared it would be very appealing to the masses, despite the fact that it was all lies and he didn't give a lick about policies.

He was manipulating them, telling them exactly what they wanted to hear, and they were eating it up. It made me want to scream at them all. But I didn't. I would've been just another story buried in the newscast, far beneath Agusto Masterson's announcement that he was in the running to become the country's savior and leader. I could even see the headline: Woman goes on a crazy rant about humanitarian CEO.

He opened the floor to a few questions that I knew had been preselected. I'd helped distribute them. The reporter from CNN went first. "What made you decide to run, Mr. Masterson?"

"A lot of things. But, in leading the charge against Zero, I realized just how much I love this nation and our people. Why not help take us to the next level of greatness?"

*The next level of greatness?* I thought to myself. It made me sick to think about how different his definition of greatness was likely to be from mine.

The next reporter read his question. "You already have some stiff competition, Mr. Masterson. So far you're the only one to announce without any political background, and since you've also announced as independent, do you realistically expect to win?"

Agusto's eyes flashed with anger, but you could have blinked and missed it. I'd seen the original question, and the reporter had editorialized it quite a bit. It was supposed to just ask how he planned to approach his candidacy against so many opponents with extensive political backgrounds.

I feared for that reporter's career, but I was glad he'd asked the question.

"Of course I expect to win. If I didn't, I wouldn't be pouring all my blood, sweat, and tears into my campaign. I'm afraid if you don't have any more intelligent questions, that'll be it for the day, folks. We'll see you on the campaign trail. Let's bring in the new year with a bang." He waved as he walked off stage, and as he passed us on his way to the door at the back of the room, he whispered into Amanda's ear, loudly enough for me to hear it. "Take care of that reporter."

She nodded once, and I hoped she didn't need help with that particular task. I did *not* want to know what he meant.

Once he was out of sight, and the reporters started clearing out, I risked talking to Amanda. "Do you think that little tantrum at the end will hurt him?"

"Not much. Only you and I know him well enough to know how angry he really was. Tread lightly if you know what's good for you."

"For how long?"

"Forever." She walked away, her posture a little stiff—

no doubt from the weight of the task on her shoulders. I didn't envy her one bit. She'd done some terrible things to me in the past, but was this really what she deserved?

I no longer believed I knew the answer to that question.

# 16

Christmas Day was a quiet affair in my apartment. I hadn't expected to have the day off, but Agusto's office was closed, so I wouldn't have to report to work. Of course, that didn't mean I wouldn't get any demanding text messages. I tried to sleep in, but I couldn't. I was used to being up first thing on Christmas morning. Maddie and I always used to wake up before her parents and count down until it was what they considered a "reasonable hour" before we started pounding on their door. The tradition had continued into our twenties, although our knocking had become more courteous, and we always came bearing coffee.

Her family had felt like my own, and it hurt me to be so alienated from them. Of course, it was for their own good—David thought it would be too dangerous for them to hear from me. Thinking about being apart from them, not to mention breaking our traditions, made me feel even worse about the day that stretched ahead.

It was my first Christmas without Maddie, and my first with a serious boyfriend, and somehow, I was lying alone in a strange apartment with an unfamiliar haircut, and I didn't even feel like I knew myself.

As I watched the clock roll over to 7 AM, I felt like crying. It was going to be a long, lonely day.

I didn't contact Owen to tell him Merry Christmas. I figured I'd let him sleep if he could. Frankly, I had no idea what his Christmas traditions were. He'd been with the Unseen for much of his childhood. Maybe they did their own thing Christmas morning.

Around 10 AM, I was flipping through a magazine in bed, trying to enjoy a cup of coffee, when someone knocked on the door.

That was all it took for me to be on full alert. No one had ever knocked on my door before. Beyond my contacts in the Unseen and the HR folks in Agusto's building, I wasn't sure anyone knew my address. Without even wasting a moment to set my coffee down, I silently reached out for the person on the other side of the door. It wasn't one person; there were four of them. Four totally unarmed nonreaders. Based on their thoughts, they were musicians.

Curious, I got up and padded across the room in my sweats and T-shirt. I grabbed a zip-up sweater off the floor near my bed and wrapped it tightly around my body to give myself a sense of security, if not decency, and opened the door.

"Can I help you?" The four men were holding string instruments—two violins, a viola, and a cello. They were dressed in tuxedos, making me feel horribly out of place in my own home.

"Joyce Nye?" asked one of the violinists.

"Yes…" I trailed off, not sure where this was going.

"May we come in? We're here to give you a private concert."

Still wary of them, I dug for more information. "Can I ask who sent you?" If it was Agusto, he knew too much about me, and that would ruin the entire performance. But if Owen had arranged for them to come here, there was a chance I would melt right then and there. Of course, I hadn't yet done anything for him. I'd figured I would get him a gift later, when I could actually celebrate with him in person.

"We aren't supposed to tell you. He said he would be in touch later to see if you enjoyed our performance."

That didn't exactly set me at ease, but as I watched the cello player shift his rather large instrument case, they didn't seem like an immediate threat. Suddenly feeling rude, I stepped aside and ushered them into the apartment. "Please, come in. But my place is awfully small. And...well, it's not the best, acoustically speaking." Embarrassed, I rushed around and started to pick up clothing that I'd tossed on the floor, but because it was a one-room apartment, I didn't really have anywhere to stash it. I shoved it under the bed, smiling sheepishly all the while. The men didn't seem to notice as they set up their stands and equipment right in front of the TV, apparently determining that it was the best spot for their performance.

But then they started playing, their instruments sending a beautifully haunting rendition of Gaspard into my apartment. I'd never heard it arranged for a string quartet before, and it carried me away as I watched their bows fly through the movements. Before I knew it, more than twenty minutes had passed, and they'd played the whole piece.

In the silence that followed the completion of their performance, they rested a moment and got their music in order. I sat with my head tilted back against the wall, one hand clutching my long-cold coffee, reveling in the aftermath of the music. I was so wrapped up in the piece that I didn't even think to clap for them.

They didn't seem to notice, or if they did, they didn't react. They proceeded to spend the next hour and a half playing a full concert for me, filled with beautiful symphonies and concertos I'd never heard solely on strings. It was a wonderfully unique experience, and it made my Christmas rather magical, even if I was alone.

When they were done, I thanked them profusely.

The lead violin player nodded. "You know, we had to learn that first piece special for you. He was very adamant that we needed to play it first thing. He said we could play whatever we wanted after that, but Gaspard de la Nuit had to come first. When he asked for it, he called it Gasbag de la Noot. It actually took us some time to figure out what he meant." He shook his head as he said it, and the comment brought tears to my eyes.

"Thank you." It was Owen. It had to be. He was the only one who called it that. I didn't think the first time was purposeful, but after that, the name had stuck—our first shared joke.

I found that I was no longer lonely after they left. Instead, I was filled with love and appreciation for the family I had found for myself.

After the holidays, the public rallied to Agusto's campaign in an unprecedented way. His new website crashed the first day it was up. My mission was starting to feel hopeless.

I'd been working for him for nearly a month, and the only thing we'd really learned—beyond what the public knew—was that he didn't have the people's or the country's best interests in mind.

Amanda and I worked around the clock to get things ready for his official campaign. Because he was running independent, the primaries didn't really apply to him. So he planned to start trying to win votes in the big states in February. Pollsters were forecasting the lowest turnout at the primaries in history. An unprecedented number of people planned to vote independent in the coming election, and everyone knew what that meant.

One day in the beginning of January, Amanda and I were cleaning up the conference room after a campaign meeting. Potential campaign slogans and sample fliers littered the room.

"The first president I actually remember is Bush. Well, the senior Bush," I said as I leaned down to pick up a stray flier that had gone under the table.

"I was upset because some of my classmates were talking about how his policies were going to leave all of our parents unemployed. We were only in second grade, and we knew nothing about presidential policies, but it was enough to make me worry. Later that day, I spoke to my a—" I stopped myself before I could get the rest of the word out. She was watching me intensely, with a look of disbelief in her eyes. I cleared my throat. "Anyway, my mom and dad were fine, and they laughed when I voiced my concerns. Kids are so weird." I chuckled uneasily as I ducked down beneath the table again, desperately searching for something to pick up, a lifeline to save me from what I'd done.

In the complete silence of the room, a chilly sense of foreboding spread over me. It had taken almost a month, but I knew I'd finally done it. I'd connected the dots for her.

I braced myself for her reaction as I stood. She'd always been the kind of person who didn't yell, and it was in those quiet moments that her wrath was the most frightening. I watched as surprise and then anger flitted across her face. "What the hell are you doing here?" she said, her tone so low and menacing, it gave me goose bumps.

"Amanda…" I trailed off, not sure what to say. Damage control, that was what I needed to do, and yet, I had no clue how I could fix this.

"You ruined my entire life. Why have you come back?"

"No need to be melodramatic. Seems like you're doing pretty well. VP of a huge company, working closely with a man who might one day be president. Sounds good to me."

Her eyes widened. "You have no idea what I've been through because of you."

"You're right, I don't. But it's all a result of the choices you've made. I'm begging you to make the right choice now." After spending so much time with her, I knew she was much weaker than me. But I didn't really want to test her either.

"Choices *I've* made? I didn't *ask* to be your guardian. I didn't *ask* to get saddled with a kid in what should have been the best years of my life. I didn't *ask* for you to kill my associate and doom me to this life of slavery."

"Is that what you are? A slave?"

"I'm certainly not what I once was." She looked so small when she said it, breaking my heart a little more.

"I tell you what, if you help me, I'm sure the Unseen could find a place for you again. Give you a better life. Two heads are always better than one. And you're closer to him than I'll probably ever be. Help us out, and we'll help you. I'm giving you a choice now."

I could feel her weak attempt to get past the outermost defenses in my mind. "You're offering me the option to jump out of the frying pan and into the fire. Why would I want to go back to the Unseen after what they did to me?"

"Because they never did you any harm."

"Is that so? And what do you call my assignment to watch after you for eighteen miserable years?"

"Wow." After all this time, she still had the power to hurt me.

"You have nowhere to go now, Mackenzie. You're surrounded by enemies. You won't get away this time." She actually believed what she was saying. The genuine smile on her face gave her away.

She closed her eyes and began an all-out attack on me. But she was so weak, her attempts at attacking me were almost sad. "Please, Amanda, reconsider the path you're going down. Don't force my hand."

She ignored me and pressed her attack, getting pushed out by my outer defenses over and over again. But she kept coming back.

The way I saw it, I had a few options. If I let her through, she would get lost in my caves. I could trap her there, walk away, and never come back, or I could kill her and try to finish the mission. Either option was pretty unappealing to me, but I didn't want to risk the distraction of attempting to communicate with David.

After I threw her out again, she sat back, sweat dripping down her forehead. "Fine, you want to play hardball? I have something that will level the playing field."

Before I could even think to act, she rushed over to the head of the conference table. Seconds after she reached under the table, I heard a telltale click, and she brought up a small, black pistol of some kind.

I'd never had a gun pointed at me, but I was a lot calmer than I imagined I'd be. I knew deep down Amanda wasn't a threat to me, armed or not. Quickly and quietly, I reached out for her mind. "Are you really going to shoot me, right here? What would Agusto say about that?" Her defenses were pitiful. Could it have always been this way? Or had they done something to weaken her? Not too long ago, she'd presented herself as such a formidable foe, but after seeing what she'd been reduced to by whatever Agusto and his minions had done to her, it was no wonder her mind had been so affected.

"I think he'd be pleased. He might even let me go."

"Let you go?" I watched as she leveled the gun at me. But I was already inside her mind. Gently, I encouraged her to put it down.

"Stop."

"I'm not interested in getting shot today, so I don't think I will."

Tears sprang to her eyes. "This is the only way."

"I've already told you that it's not," I said calmly, trying again to reason with her.

"You don't understand." Desperation took her voice up a few notches.

"Then help me to."

Her hand fell limply to her side, letting the gun dangle, and I was bombarded with memories, starting way back when David had first asked her to take me in.

"She can't know you're a reader. I don't want her to know about this world. She must be kept safe. You're one of our most skilled readers. I'm counting on you."

"I'm not a mother, David." She frowned down at my tiny body, clutched awkwardly in her arms. "And I'm not suited to be a single parent. I like being on my own too much. This isn't the right assignment for me." She held me out to him. "I can't do this. Please, find someone else."

"There is no one else. She'll die if you don't."

"What kind of life will she have if I do? I won't love her, David. I can't. I hate her already for what I'm being asked to do for her." Her honesty was brutal, but I was gratified to know she'd fought for my best interests, if only that one time.

"There is no one else." He said it slow, and the memory faded. Next were flashes of her transition to the Potestas, my capture, my imprisonment, and then the memories slowed to focus on the time just after my escape.

"Dylan?" He'd gone limp in his chair and fallen to the floor. "No. You're our only connection to the girl. No. Fight! You can't do this to me. I'm as good as dead. You have to fight. Think of your wife, your little boy. Fight, damn you!" she cried, but it was too late. I'd already crushed that last memory. And he died at her feet.

Next, she was in darkness. The pressure she felt on her wrists, combined with the difficulty she had breathing, made me think she was hanging by her wrists, but I couldn't see anything. Obviously, she'd been beaten, but she didn't seem to remember. Pain radiated through her from head to toe.

"Well. I'd hoped we would see each other again under different circumstances, Amanda." I recognized Agusto's voice immediately, although I didn't see him. There was darkness everywhere. Maybe she had her eyes closed.

*What is he doing here? Why is the leader here to see me?* she thought.

The shock of that revelation almost made me lose my connection with her, but I held it tight.

"Didn't you like to tell that girl she was a disappointment? Now who's the disappointment?"

He hit her hard across the face, but it didn't compare to the pain she was already feeling.

"I should kill you. But you don't deserve mercy from me." His footsteps echoed in the room, and I heard him circle around behind her. "No," he whispered in her ear. "I'll keep you close to me from now on. That way I can remind you of your transgression. Regularly."

*No wonder she's so exhausted and weak,* I thought, feeling nothing but sorrow for her.

But she was still fighting me. I tried to plant a seed in her mind that would convince her to help me and rejoin the Unseen, but she fought, with all that she had left, she fought me.

I looked over at her, and she had a feral quality in her eyes. "I'm done," she said.

"I forgive you, Amanda. For everything. I hope you can forgive me too."

"See you in hell, Mackenzie." With her last ounce of willpower, she brought the gun to her head and pulled the trigger.

# 17

She'd done it so quickly, and with such determination. It was like she'd seen it as her chance to reclaim some of the strength she once had for one final deed that she could call her own.

The sound of the gunshot still rang in my ear as I dialed 911 and listened to it ring once, twice. *Come on.*

"Nine-one-one, what is your emergency?" a calm woman asked.

"My coworker just shot herself. She's not breathing. I need help right away." The alarm in my voice was real as I gave her the address, and she assured me help would be there soon.

I eyed Amanda, slumped in her chair, blood pouring out of her wound. "There's so much blood. How can I help her?" I knew I was in deep with an already-suspicious boss, who was also apparently the leader of the Potestas rather than a second or third in command like we'd assumed. The water was getting deeper all the time, and I was struggling to keep my head above it. All I could think of was creating a record of my efforts to save Amanda, something solid so I could reasonably deny involvement. It was a thin chance, but I was desperate.

Before the operator could answer me, two of Agusto's guards came in to the conference room, waving their own guns around before pointing them at me.

"Amanda shot herself," I shouted at them. "I'm on the phone with 911." Then I kicked the gun that had fallen to the floor just beneath Amanda's dangling hand toward them to demonstrate the fact that I wasn't armed.

"Are you all right?" the 911 operator asked.

How could I answer that? Two of the enemy's armed guards had their weapons aimed at me, and they hadn't relaxed their grip one bit.

"Help is on the way, guys. Calm down," I said to the guards, ignoring the operator. I knew the two men. They weren't readers. I could easily make them lower their weapons, but if I did, my cover would probably be blown. But if I didn't do anything, they might shoot me.

"Ma'am. What's going on?" the operator asked again.

"Two of the CEO's guards have come in to assess the situation. They seem to think I'm armed in some way. But I'm *not*." At least it would be on record that two armed men had aimed their weapons at an unarmed woman. That would make for a great headline for Agusto's campaign.

We eyed each other, and slowly, they lowered their weapons. For several seconds, we just stood there in a silent stand-off, and then the operator said, "Are you there?"

"Yes."

"The EMTs are in the building. They will be there shortly. Just hold on a bit longer."

"Thank you," I said, and I truly meant it.

When the EMTs arrived, they stepped around the guards, totally ignoring them, making the guards move off to the side. They tried to shock Amanda a few times, but it didn't help. After what seemed like an eternity, they loaded her onto a gurney, leaving nothing but a bloody mess behind.

One of them approached me. "You're the one who

called?"

Nodding was the only thing I could bring myself to do. The ramifications of what had unfolded weighed heavily on me. Despite the fact that I hadn't pulled the trigger, I couldn't help but feel responsible. I'd spent most of my life with Amanda, and although I still didn't feel any love for her, I felt sorry for the role I'd played in her death.

"I'm sure the police will have some questions for you." The EMT startled me out of my inner thoughts. "We were never able to get a heartbeat. I'm sorry." He put a hand on my shoulder, squeezed, and left.

As he walked out, I noticed a huge crowd had gathered outside the doorway of the conference room. Police officers were keeping them back, and I eyed their vacant expressions. As I realized they were being controlled, I spotted Agusto and understood why. He was keeping them away from me so he could have me all to himself. He gave me a hard look before turning and walking away. The crowd parted for him, and I knew I was supposed to follow. My mind and heart rebelled against the idea of following him, but my feet did as they were told. People watched us as we went, but I didn't make eye contact. I couldn't worry about what they thought. I needed to focus on surviving whatever happened next.

As we walked down the hall to his office, I risked sending a quick message to David.

*Amanda dead. Agusto number one. Going to his office now.* Then I buried my signature as deeply as I could. I had no idea what Agusto was capable of doing, and I didn't want to risk exposing our headquarters to literally all the Potestas. It would mean the end of us for sure, and without our protection, the people of our country would be at their mercy. As it stood, I was fairly certain this little exchange would be the end of me. There was no need for others to share my fate.

The two guards who'd interrupted my call for help fell in on either side of Agusto as we drew closer to his office.

Just a few more feet and I'd be closed into a room with five guards and him. Six-to-one odds.

My mind reeled as I followed him into the office. I glanced around for some kind of safety rope to pull me out of the pit of quicksand I'd tumbled into, but there was nothing. Anyway, I wasn't sure what I expected to find. I had no allies in this building. They were all a few miles away, safely within our headquarters. Well, all except for our mole, and I had no idea who that person even was.

Once I was inside, the door closed loudly behind me. Agusto was already making his way toward his desk, so I followed, eying the guards as they took their places along the wall. I knew two of them weren't readers, including one of the ones standing closest to Agusto.

But before I could form a plan, Agusto spoke to me. "Tell me exactly what happened."

My voice was shaky as I gave him the details. "We got to talking while we were cleaning up the room after the campaign meeting. I don't even know what set her off, but the conversation turned south. She said something about being a failure and feeling trapped...and...and then she pulled a gun out from under the table and shot herself. It all happened so fast. I called nine-one-one, but they arrived too late to help her." I hoped that by telling him most of the truth, it would seem believable. After all, I hadn't lied; I just hadn't told him the whole story. But the thought of her with the gun pressed to her head set the room spinning. But instead of sitting down or steadying myself in any way, I straightened my spine and swallowed the bile in the back of my throat.

"And that was that?" His tone was flat and hard to read, making me even more hyper-aware of the precarious situation I was in.

"Except for the part where your two lackeys came in and tried to shoot me, yes."

"That *is* unfortunate," he said, ignoring my comment about his lackeys. "I now find myself without a campaign manager. Despite the fact that Amanda was a bit of a blundering idiot, she was loyal." He turned his chair around, mumbling to himself. "Not out of respect, but out of fear. Fear makes people reliably loyal. Respect can be taken away at any moment, but fear..." He trailed off as he considered his options. "But who could replace her?"

As he tried to work through his problem, I took another assessment of the situation. *Could I get into his mind while he's distracted?* A quick glance at the closest guard made me hesitate. If he suspected anything at all, it would be over for me.

*If I can just keep him talking. Keep him distracted.* I would need to speak to Agusto while making my attack on his mind, and I'd need to keep broadcasting nothing thoughts to trick his attack dogs. Sure, I'd managed to multi-task with Amanda, but she had been relatively weak. Surely their number one would be a formidable foe.

Agusto was still mumbling about his options, and what to do, while I felt time running out. I couldn't stand there forever.

It was now or never.

# 18

"What about Bob Yarwick? He worked closely with Amanda on a few projects," I said, trying to keep Agusto distracted. Bob worked downstairs, but I didn't actually know what his title was. He seemed to be one of Amanda's go-to people for getting things done for the campaign. I had no idea if he was a good candidate or not. At the moment, his best interests weren't foremost in my thoughts. Keeping Agusto talking was job number one.

"No. He's an idiot. Too much of a yes man. He'd be crushed by the politics of this. In fact, why does he even work for us? I should fire him immediately."

I nodded, my mind too busy trying to find a way to survive this mess to worry about Bob Yarwick and the fact that he was about to be unemployed. I tried to come up with other names, but as it turned out, he didn't need that much prodding to keep talking.

I looked absently out the wall of windows and turned my focus inward, feeling like it was time to act. I split my concentration so I would keep hearing the audio of what was happening in the "real" world in the forefront of my mind.

Not bothering to risk another glance at the guards, I

pressed my mental attack, but I couldn't find him. He was sitting right smack in front of me, and yet his psychic space was like a black hole.

*Maybe I've lost my touch,* I thought as I reached out for the guards, all of whom I located easily.

I listened to him as he combed through his options again and again. His mind was running a mile a minute, so he should've been easy to find. He was practically screaming at me. But he just wasn't there. Over and over, I tried to find him; each time, I was met with nothing. Not even darkness or a wall, like I was used to seeing in protected minds, just nothing. Like the man in front of me wasn't a living thing at all. It made me feel even more desperate.

I'd already reached out for the guards, potentially alerting them to what I was doing. Time was ticking away while I floundered in front of the leader of the Potestas. I had the potential to end their organization right then there, but I couldn't tap into the mind of the man sitting right in front of me.

"You." He interrupted my thoughts and brought me slamming back into myself rather uncomfortably.

Clearing my throat, I struggled to respond. "Excuse me?"

"You. It has to be you." He smiled at me, as if he'd found the perfect solution.

"What?" A feeling of dread filled me at his suggestion. He'd zeroed in on me for a reason. None of Joyce's qualifications pointed toward her being a logical choice for campaign manager. He was angling toward something. But what? Was he just trying to keep me off kilter, so I couldn't press my mental attack, or was there more to it?

In the silence that followed, I listened to the bubbling of the river, which created a false sense of peace. It was nothing close to peaceful in there. Calm, yes, but in a sinister way that let me know he could kill me at any moment and feel absolutely no regrets about it.

As his eyes bored into me, my discomfort grew. "You heard me. I know you haven't worked for me long, but I can already tell you're perfect for the job. You're already very involved in the campaign, so you know what needs to be done. You'd need minimal training. And, I tell you what, I'll hire someone to replace you, so you'll have help."

Desperate to stall him, I fumbled for something to say, anything at all that would keep him talking for long enough for me to make another effort. But what if I was doomed to act as his second in command for the rest of my life, never being able to escape back to the Unseen?

I took a deep breath and scolded myself. *Stop it. You're being melodramatic. They know who he is. They'll get to work. All you need to do is hang in there.*

"I can see that you're overwhelmed with gratitude. No need to thank me now." He turned his back to me. "Go, gather your things, and get settled into Amanda's office, I mean *your* office." He turned around and smiled at me.

I knew I couldn't take him at his word, but I wasn't sure what to do. *Just keep him talking,* I thought.

"Perhaps you'd like to go over some of the details of my duties, since Amanda never shared that kind of thing with me."

"I don't think that's a valuable way to spend my time right now. In fact…" He trailed off and nodded to one of the guards. The man approached, keeping his eyes glued on me.

"The campaign manager is someone I need to keep very close. I know you are going to be well suited for the post. Do you know why?"

Instead of responding, I watched as the other four guards slowly closed in on us. The final guard stood close to Agusto's side, and I knew we were getting to the meat of what he had in mind.

Despite my best efforts to stay calm, my heart was racing, my breath coming in short gasps. I was probably visibly sweating, but I didn't want to bring my hand to my forehead to find out. No need to draw further attention to my distress.

*I need to abort this, right now,* I thought.

"You know what? It's been a very stressful day. I think I'll leave you to it, and I'll get to work on figuring out where Amanda left off," I said. So much for seizing the moment; I was in survival mood. "At any rate, I think the police were waiting to speak to me."

I took a half step back, but he stopped me. "You're not going anywhere. You didn't answer my question. Don't you want to know why I need to keep you close?"

I shook my head as the guards continued to close in on me. Soon, Agusto was on one end of the circle of guards, and I was on the other—surrounded. The two guards closest to me could've seized me in an instant.

"Because you keep your friends close, but you keep your enemies closer."

# 19

Swallowing hard, I tried to keep my cool. "I don't know what you're talking about."

He glared at me, and his tone turned so cold, I was surprised I couldn't see his breath. "Don't lie to me. I can smell a liar from fifty yards away. Call it one of my talents."

*His talents? He was a one-man lie detector in addition to being able to read minds? Well, all bow down to the great and powerful Oz,* I thought, secretly hoping he heard me.

"Tell me, what are your other talents? Maybe we should be exploiting them for your campaign."

"I believe you know full well what they are, not to mention who I am."

"You believe? Shouldn't you know without a doubt? Seems to me your talents are less impressive than they should be given that you're the leader of the Potestas."

His smile was vicious. "Now we're getting somewhere." He took a step toward me, and the circle around us got smaller. The air was close, and I struggled to keep my panic at bay. "How long have you known who I am?"

"I think part of me suspected it all along. Maybe a

better question is do you know who I am?" I was getting antsy. This back and forth had gone on for too long. Someone was going to draw soon, and if I wanted to win, it needed to be me. All I had to do was find his mind—a task easier said than done.

"I know you're a member of the Unseen, and a thorn in my side. And I know that I'm going to crush you, and the rest of your sad little organization, one by one."

Internally, I breathed a sigh of relief. He had no idea specifically who I was.

"Now that we're being honest with each other, tell me how you managed to get as far as you did. How did a little worm like you get so close to me?"

"With a little bit of skill and a lot of luck." *No need to elaborate*, I thought. If I didn't make it out of here alive, at least he wouldn't have any useful information. Of course, if he was as powerful as he believed himself to be, he could probably get everything he wanted out of me, whether I was willing or not. Still, I wasn't giving him anything for free.

I glanced at the guard to Agusto's right, and immediately wished I hadn't. He was glaring at me so hard it was almost comical. The look in his eyes was what kept me from laughing. Stone cold and deadly. I found I had a hard time looking away.

"What gave me away?" I asked, still trying to find a way out of this as I tore my gaze away from the angry guard.

He chuckled. "You're dumber than I thought, Mackenzie."

I opened my mouth to respond, but my breath caught in my throat. He'd called me Mackenzie, not Joyce. *That lying sack of shit! He knows exactly who I am.*

Anger and panic kept my heart racing as a smile spread across his face. "Yes. Amanda wore a wire at all times. I heard your entire exchange. Your slip up. Her realization of who you were. Her refusal to accept your offer of rescue. Her cowardly death. It was better than she deserved." His last statement was so oddly matter-of-fact. I knew beyond a shadow of a doubt he meant it, and I didn't want to take the time to imagine exactly what kind of end he would've given her.

"And now my little sheep has wandered back into the wolf's den on her own." He paused and his smile made me nauseous. "Although, I must congratulate you on keeping yourself hidden from the person who raised you. She should've known you inside and out. It seems Amanda was a bigger imbecile than I thought."

"That's a bit of a backhanded compliment," I said.

Agusto nodded in acknowledgment, staring at me intently. I could tell it was a challenge, but I wasn't sure I could be intimidated any further. I was already scared out of my mind.

The guard to Agusto's right, the one who who'd been glaring at me only moments ago, cleared his throat. When I looked at him, his once-fierce glare seemed vacant. His expression was more relaxed. Confused, I turned back to Agusto, not wanting to draw attention to the guard's apparent transformation. As far as I was concerned, he was one less person for me to worry about.

Not seeming to notice what was going on with the guard, Agusto continued to revel in his success in capturing me.

"You thought you'd come in here and expose me for the demon I am, hmm? That's very heroic of you." He turned and started walking toward the window, breaking our little circle. It gave me some space to breathe, to think.

"What do you plan to do with me now?" I asked, stalling.

"Oh…" He trailed off wistfully. "There are so many options. You could become my new Amanda, but I don't think you'd allow yourself to become a prisoner to your fear, particularly since we tried imprisoning you once before. Your talents are so…extensive, I'd hate to waste them. But make no mistake, I will if you force my hand."

"I believe you." I may have gotten myself into some pretty deep trouble, but I wasn't stupid.

He smiled broadly as he looked out the window. "Maybe you're not as dumb as I thought." His breath fogged the window as he looked out on the county's monuments.

I followed his gaze. "Do you envision having a monument to your greatness out there some day?"

He laughed. It was a genuine belly laugh, not an I'm-humoring-you chuckle. "Of course not. This country will be too busy to spend time on such frivolity. In fact—"

The guard to his left cleared his throat, cutting him off. Agusto glanced at him, an annoyed expression on his face, before looking away. "In fact, I'm going to change the face of this nation in such a way—"

A third guard cleared his throat, and then a fourth. Finally, the fifth guard started all-out coughing. "I'm sorry, am I boring you, boys? Do you have something to say? Or do you just need a drink? Feel free to drink from the river, like the dogs you are."

My gaze bounced between them. Were they signaling each other? If so, why didn't Agusto know what they were doing? Upon further inspection, I realized they all shared the same vacant expression.

*What the hell's going on?* I wondered.

Before I could process anything, the original guard who'd glared at me took Agusto into a defensive hold, keeping his arms pinned behind his back.

"What are you doing?" Agusto bellowed.

"Now's your chance," the guard said, looking right at me.

# 20

Questions raced through my mind. *What if it's a trap? What if they've designed this, and they plan on imprisoning me once I'm inside his mind?* But I couldn't dilly-dally. I couldn't waste this opportunity. Instead of voicing any of the millions of questions racing through my head, I shut my eyes, giving myself the chance to fully focus on the task at hand.

I was taking a huge risk by opening myself to the four other guards flanking me, but I had to put my trust in something.

Doubling down, I concentrated on breaking into Agusto's head. He struggled against the guard, and I could distantly hear the other guards moving away from me—moving toward him. "I don't know what you think you're doing, but it'll never work. I'm the leader of the damn Potestas. You can't get into my head."

I easily found the mind of the guard who was pinning Agusto, but he felt different this time, almost familiar.

"Hurry up, Mackenzie. Don't waste any time."

I could've just killed him. I eyed the guard holding Agusto, wondering where he kept his gun, but I decided against it. Agusto had too much information. We needed to know where the Potestas' supply of Zero was being kept, where they planned to release it next, how big the organization was, and how deep it went. The questions were endless, and this one man held all the answers.

I made another effort to find Agusto. There was still only the void. "What are you, some kind of robot?" I said out of frustration. Agusto laughed, and I heard him stop struggling.

"You'll never be able to find your way inside my mind."

"Don't bet on it," I said, trying to think fast. The guard was so close to the void that I could almost feel it, feel *him*, but almost wasn't good enough.

"You three, can you get closer to him?" I pointed to the three guards separating me from Agusto.

That left one standing at my side. "Maybe you should watch the door?" He nodded and walked stiffly to the door. That still left Amanda's secret door unguarded, but it was a risk I had to take at the moment.

"Okay good. One on each side, please?" I asked the guards, and they positioned themselves around him.

Closing my eyes again, I tightened my focus. The void was so obvious now, but I had no idea how to penetrate it. With four minds on all sides of him, it felt almost like a black hole of nothing in the middle of so much activity.

As I got closer to finding him, I heard him start to struggle again. His laugh changed from confident to slightly nervous. "You'll never find me. My defenses are flawless. They were created by the best readers in the world."

"Created?" I asked, coming back to myself.

But the original guard holding him begged me to keep working. "We don't have much time, Mackenzie. He's just trying to distract you, and it's working. Keep going."

But the phrase bothered me. Why would his defenses have been created by some of the best mind readers in the world? I thought about Dr. Jeppe. His defenses had been created for him too, but his had been almost laughably bad. This was something different. It was a work of art, as far as defenses were concerned. To another reader, Agusto didn't exist. How had he accomplished that? Or rather, how had someone else accomplished that for him?

And, more importantly, why would someone else need to accomplish that for the leader of the Potestas?

I looked at him, desperately flailing as he tried to escape the guards. "You're not a reader." It was a statement, not a question.

In that moment he stopped struggling and got very still. A smile crept its way across my face as I let that truth reveal him to me.

He was a fraud.

Tracy's words came back to me one last time. *Reality is a fluid concept in the world of the mind. It's real because your mind believes it to be.* His defenses weren't real. Creative to be sure, but they were nothing but lies. And there was nothing inside of him with the ability to bolster them.

The truth spread away from me, like roots reaching for him, pulling away the void with its tendrils. "The truth will set you free, Agusto," I said with a smile as I started to feel him.

Then, all at once, I knew everything.

I had always assumed the Potestas had existed for generations. But I was wrong. The Potestas had popped up fairly recently, started by a young Agusto Masterson and his best friend, a rather talented and sadistic reader gone rogue from the Unseen.

I watched as they slowly gained followers over time, ones like Washington, who staunchly supported their cause and justified their means to an end, and others like Amanda, who got in over their heads and became too afraid to leave. They made empty promises, meaningful threats, anything they could to attract supporters.

Agusto was extremely charismatic, as I already knew, but his friend wasn't. He was creepy, and people shied away from him. Agusto felt they were losing too many readers to his attitude, so he approached him about adopting a softer approach. His friend refused. Agusto persisted, saying it was for the greater good, and implored him to think of their dream, their bigger picture.

They wanted so badly to overthrow the Unseen. They'd reprimanded Agusto's friend for his sadistic ways, prompting his AWOL status, and he'd never forgotten or forgiven it. For him, taking over the world one step at a time was no more than bonus. It was necessary because of the number and variety of Unseen chapters across the world.

But Agusto disagreed. For him, felling the Unseen was no more than an excuse for him to gain the power he'd always wanted.

It ended in a fight, leaving Agusto's best friend, the only person with whom he'd shared a meaningful relationship, dead. Somehow, it surprised me that Agusto didn't seem to feel any remorse over the act. In fact, he seemed *pleased* that he wouldn't have to share his empire with anyone else.

After that, I flashed forward a decade, maybe two, and watched him hatch the idea of Zero. He gave the project to Dylan Shields and their newest—and most promising—recruit, Amanda, who in turn recruited the members they would need to successfully complete the project. It was hard to see Amanda so full of life. She'd been so pumped, so excited about the new direction her life was taking.

But it all crumbled as I watched. He tortured her for information, trying to piece together how one of their most valuable assets had slipped through his fingers. He struggled to understand what it meant for him, and whether it would affect the success of his plan.

And I saw his plan laid out in front of me, like blueprints. He didn't intend to stop once he was declared president of the U.S. After all these years, he was a patient man. Slowly but surely, he would extend his tentacles out into the world, taking it over country by country, until he had control of all the world's resources. His terrorist tactics wouldn't end with Zero. He would buy a weapons company to help fuel the wars in the Middle East—not only supporting, but also controlling groups like ISIS. And then he planned to take control of the world's economy by bending the oil companies to his whim, driving the cost of gas up so high that no one would be able to afford to drive anywhere, halting transport of all kind until he said go. All in the name of bringing down the Unseen for a perceived wrong that wasn't even his to claim.

It was a nightmare, a living nightmare. Once everything he knew was out in the open, I didn't know what to do. Slowly, I came back to myself, but I almost collapsed right there. The urge to fall to my knees from total and utter hopelessness was overwhelming.

The guards looked at me, waiting, and I had no idea what to do. They were all still holding him, and Agusto was staring at me, knowing he'd been violated. His eyes were wide, frantic, and feral. But now that I knew him for who he was, his fear didn't bother me a bit.

"I thought you hated liars," I said. He didn't respond. "You're one of the worst liars of all. You don't have any special talent, except maybe the power of deception."

"Do you have what you need?" asked the guard who had restrained him first.

I nodded, and he reached around and took Agusto in a hold by the neck. Before too long, he collapsed into unconsciousness. Then, just like that, the three guards around him fell to the ground, as did the guard at the door, leaving the original guard the only one standing.

He was looking directly at me.

# 21

Stunned, I stared the original guard down, not sure what he had in mind at this point. Was he still an ally of sorts? Before I could make a move, he spoke to me.

"Well, you people have really managed to pull something off here, haven't you?" His eyes were clearing. Blind rage replaced the vacancy I'd seen there only moments ago.

"Who are you?" I asked, still reeling.

"Someone who's stronger than these other guards, apparently." He reached around behind him, and I knew he was going for his gun. I had to act fast, but I was tired of being on my toes, tired of trying to stay one step ahead of all these people who were trying to kill me.

The lag hurt me, and before I could stop him, he leveled his weapon at me. "Enough mental games. This ends right here, right now."

The door opened behind us, and he looked over my shoulder.

A shot rang out, and I screamed. I'd been shot. Even though I felt nothing, I knew that one of the enemies who'd surrounded me for weeks must have finally ended my life. It had to be shock or something that was blocking out the pain. I thought of Owen, David, Maddie, and Mitchell in those long, taut moments.

Then the feeling of a hand clasping my shoulder brought me back to the world, back to that office where bodies were strewn around the floor. One more lay at my feet with a gunshot wound in his head.

I braced myself to see an enemy as I turned around. But it wasn't an enemy at all, and I threw myself into his open arms.

"Daddy," I breathed into his chest as he hugged me close to him.

"It's okay. Everything is okay now," he said, but I wasn't sure which one of us he was trying to reassure. He pulled back, and I saw Owen waiting in the doorway, along with Mitchell, Rebecca, and Camden—one for each guard.

*No wonder the guards felt so familiar,* I thought as I surveyed my rescuers.

"How did you guys get in?" I asked, almost breathless.

"Very carefully. The police milling around due to Amanda's untimely death presented an added challenge, but they've dispersed now, with some...ahem...encouragement. Mitchell's been working on disassembling their security for weeks in the event of a storm-the-castle approach. Thanks to him, we didn't have to worry about pesky things like cameras and keycards," David answered, and all I could do was smile. They had been there for me when it mattered most. All along, they'd been keeping me safe from behind the scenes.

David released me and I went to Owen, feeling like laughing and crying all at once. Mitchell didn't let me fall apart.

"We don't have all day for emotional reunions, Mac. Need I remind you that we're in enemy territory?"

Glancing back at Agusto, I saw him stirring. "Why didn't you kill him too?"

"He's our proof," David said. "We need him. You can't be the only one who knows who, and what, he is. As long as he has information about the Potestas and Zero, he's valuable."

As he said it, an idea occurred to me. "He's also our getaway."

Now that Agusto's defenses had been obliterated, I infiltrated Agusto's mind easily. I even found I could do so while easily maintaining control of myself. I walked him out in front of me, and then followed him out of his office. The rest of our group followed silently behind.

We made our way to the elevator, and I held my breath as the doors opened. We were reentering a world that didn't know what had just happened.

We were careful not to make eye contact as we made our way out of the building and onto the street, but no one even looked our way. Everyone was so afraid of Agusto that we easily exited enemy territory and reentered neutral ground.

We got into three separate cabs, keeping Agusto with David and me, and made our way back to headquarters.

The receptionist recognized him right away. "Mr. Masterson," she said, "what a surprise. It's a pleasure to have you here. What can we do for you?"

But David showed her his ID and waved her off. It was the closest we'd come to being stopped.

Given the time of day, the building was frustratingly populated. So, Mitchell and a few of the others took charge of making people feel like they had somewhere else to be, giving us an opportunity to gain entry to our headquarters.

Not knowing where else to go, I took him to the main conference room. It was the only private place that was big enough for all of us. Davis was already there.

"Yes, Mr. President. I assure you, we have our best men and women on the case." He looked up at us and smiled when he saw Agusto. "And as it happens, they've returned with quite the spoils of war, I must say."

"Agusto Masterson was indeed a master of deception," the report declared, documentary style. It had only been a few hours since his apprehension, but word had spread like wildfire, fanned by some well-placed members of the Unseen.

"Though he was charismatic and loved by the public, most of his employees have come forward to say they were terrified of him, and had received numerous threats from him or his vice president, Amanda Pierce, who died suspiciously in his office earlier today.

"Now that Masterson is in custody, the full scope of his plan is finally coming to light. But here's what we know: Masterson was the head of a huge terrorist organization. That organization was in fact responsible for the attacks using Zero." The reporter paused for dramatic effect while a slideshow of muted video clips and file photos of Agusto played in the background. "It seems the former presidential candidate wasn't working to protect the world from Zero after all—he was the cause of it. Details are still pouring in about this shocking revelation involving the world's self-proclaimed savior."

The slideshow ended, returning viewers to the newsroom, where the anchors transitioned to a similar story. "In related news, Masterson's main office building in Washington DC was raided today, resulting in over one hundred and fifty arrests. No injuries have been reported, as most employees are said to have gone with officers quietly."

"But not all of them were guilty, David. Some of them weren't even readers at all. They didn't know what was going on; they were just trying to earn a living," I protested as the frame showed droves of people being led away in handcuffs.

"The innocent will be sorted out, I promise."

Nodding, I turned my attention back to the television.

"Masterson is currently being held behind bars

without bail, while authorities gather evidence against him. Nationally, he is currently facing first-degree murder charges for the attack on Coda, the international music festival held in Tallahassee, Florida, last fall. Internationally, it appears he will face a myriad of charges, as the nations wait to take their shot at this outed terrorist."

"What does that mean?" I asked, wrinkling my nose at the jargon.

"It means they're not ready to divulge all the charges they're going to throw at him, but they have to charge him with something in order to hold him."

I sat back in my chair, relishing the feeling of being surrounded by my family, and reached out for Owen's hand. It felt so good to be back with them, to be myself again. No one was pretending any more, at least not until the next mission. "Now what? Do we at least get to take a vacation before the next crazy person decides to kill everyone on Earth?"

David smiled at me, and I felt Owen take my left hand and slip a ring onto my finger. I looked at the ring—a rose gold swirl of diamonds. After studying it for a few moments, I realized it was a sideways treble cleft. I peered into his deep brown eyes, so filled with love, and knew I was finally home.

"Now, we live," he said.

# EPILOGUE

I sat at the piano, my dress spilling over the back of the bench, the riot of lace and pearls resting in the grass at my feet. I'd always wanted to play outside, and what better occasion than our wedding?

Owen sat next to me on the bench, watching my hands dance across the keys as I effortlessly played Gaspard de la Nuit for him, and only him, despite the guests who sat at a distance. It was the concert of my life.

Gaspard possessed me, surrounding us both, and even though I looked into Owen's eyes rather than at the keys, I didn't miss a single note. Tears filled both of our eyes as I finished the long piece. Perhaps our guests were bored, but I didn't care. This wasn't for them. It was for us. It felt like the end of one chapter of our lives and the beginning of something new and beautiful.

As the spring breeze carried the notes away, I couldn't help but let the joy I felt bubble out of me as I threw my arms around my new husband.

I was not alone at the piano, and I never would be again.

# ACKNOWLEDGEMENTS

First, and foremost, I need to thank God. I am blown away by this journey, and the blessings we've received along the way. Thank You so much. Even in the tough times, God is good, every day.

To my wonderful husband: Can you believe it? We made it! The trilogy is finished! Congratulations go to him as much as they do to me, because he has been such an awesome help. He's been involved in everything from bouncing ideas off each other to handling the marketing of the series, as well as the business end of things. You are my rock when I wonder if this is all worth it. Thank you. I wouldn't be here without you.

To Shannon Mayer, my dear friend and colleague. It's your fault *The Dead World* isn't being published right now, and I think a lot of my readers are very grateful for that. You are such a constant inspiration, and motivator. Thank you for being in my life.

To my awesome team—Angela, Cynthia, and Damonza—what would I do without you? You all make my books what they are, each with your own touch. They are perfect because of you. I love getting to my publication date, and saying there isn't a darn thing I would change about this book. And that happens every time. It's magic that I am so thankful to be a part of.

My friends, Christian, Mary, and Dannie, I love you. You relentlessly ride the ups and downs with me, and for that, I am forever grateful. Hold on tight! I think this ride is only going to get more fun!

To my family, Mom, Dad, Shane, you guys are amazing supporters. Thank you for reading my books and telling literally everyone you know, and a lot of people you don't know, including a lot of radio listeners in Connecticut, about my books. Love you guys!

That leaves me with you, dear reader. You've stayed with me through this entire series. That's quite a commitment, and for that, I think you are Awesome, with a capital A. Thank you so much for sacrificing your time to spend it with my characters and me. I truly appreciate it, more than I can say.

Until December guys, happy reading!

—S

# ABOUT THE AUTHOR

Stephanie Erickson is an English Literature graduate from Flagler College. She lives in Florida with her family. Undivided is her sixth novel.

She loves to connect with readers! Follow her on Facebook at http://www.facebook.com/stephmerickson, Twitter @sm_erickson, or stop by her Web site at www.stephanieericksonbooks.com.

You can also get the latest news on new releases, contests, and author appearances by signing up for her newsletter on her Web site.

# BOOK LIST

CPSIA information can be obtained at www.ICGtesting.com
Printed in the USA
LVOW11s0346171215

466948LV00002B/268/P